Joyful Gospel Stories

Previously, Meanwhile, and Subsequently

Michael Holsten

Dedication

These stories are dedicated to the gracious people in Phoenix, Arizona and in Tralee and Dublin, Ireland who have encouraged and blessed me and my wife, Rita.

Contents

Preface

Many years ago, I had the idea of stepping into a Bible story to see what was happening before the part we read, to see what was going on at the same time, and to find out what happened afterward. So, in this book, I looked for some people that might have been present in a Bible story and considered how their experience with Jesus might have touched their lives and brought them joy.

I hope these stories will bring joy to your heart and bring you closer to Jesus.

Michael Holsten

1 What Happened?

Yes, Sandor thought, it was a good day to be in the temple. He walked through the court of the Gentiles, having some sense of satisfaction that there were quite a few Gentiles there to honor the Lord. He would like to have seen more women in the next court, but he knew he was in a minority on that subject.

After finding a place in the men's court where he was satisfied, Sandor waited to see who was chosen by lot to enter the temple with the incense today. Why! it's Zacharias, he realized! Zacharias and Elizabeth lived only a short distance from his house. He hadn't seen Zacharias serve in a long time. In fact, he thought, Zacharias was getting to the age when he might retire from active serving.

Sandor had always felt sorry for Zacharias and Elizabeth. They had no children. There was no son to follow in his father's footsteps, serving in the temple. Too late now, though. Well, it was great to see Zacharias serve again.

All right, there he goes into the temple. Now, to wait for him to come out and pronounce the blessing on us all, Sandor thought.

So he waited.

After several minutes had passed, Sandor turned to the man next to him with a questioning look. His neighbor agreed that it seemed to be taking a very long time.

Again, they waited.

It seemed like quite a while later when Zacharias appeared from the temple, and there was an audible sigh of relief from those present. Then, what?! Zacharias' mouth was moving, but there was no sound coming out. Sandor looked at Zacharias' face, and it was a mixture of color-drained fear and amazed wonder.

It was a few days later when Sandor visited Zacharias and Elizabeth. Ought to at least check and see if everything's all right, he thought. Elizabeth welcomed him into their home, but there was a sense of sadness in her welcome. "He thinks he saw an angel", she told him. "And something crazy about us having a son." Her voice trailed off.

Sandor could tell she had very mixed feelings about this. What a wonderful blessing! What an impossible idea! And why, at this late time in their lives, would God open a new beginning, when they were pretty well focused on planning for the ending of this life that they had enjoyed together?

Sandor tried to communicate with Zacharias, but it was difficult. When he mentioned that Elizabeth had told him about thinking that he had seen an angel though, Zacharias got very excited. He became so agitated that Elizabeth suggested Sandor come back another time, to let Zacharias rest for a while.

Sandor was a little nervous about going back, and it got to be several weeks before he thought about going back. He asked some of the other neighbors how the two were doing. That's when he got a real shock. "Didn't you know?" one neighbor said. Old Elizabeth, bless her heart, is actually expecting. Sandor's eyes opened up wide, "You mean expecting, as in a baby?!" "That's it," said the neighbor. "Who would have thought." Right, thought Sandor. Who would have thought. Then he began to wonder what actually happened that day in the temple.

When he got to their house, there were some changes. Elizabeth's sadness and all sense of worry were gone. She absolutely glowed. She looked very much younger. Zacharias' appearance of frustration was gone. His excitement was quieter, but continuous. He looked like he was expecting something great to happen. Well, I suppose, thought Sandor, having a son, finally, would be great. But when he talked to Zacharias about it, he just smiled and shook his head. He made signs that communicated to Sandor, "Wait. Just wait and see."

On the way home, Sandor wasn't sure if he was more comforted or disturbed by the way things were turning out. During the next months, he saw Elizabeth a few times in town, but he was hesitant to go back and visit Zacharias.

Then the day finally came! Everyone in town had been on edge, to see it finally happen, that this old, wonderful couple would finally be blessed. There had even been a young woman visiting from up north who was apparently waiting for this event to happen, too. But she had left just a week ago. Now the baby had been born, and sure enough, it was a son!

It was quite a surprise when Sandor got the invitation, though. He was invited to the celebration of the naming of Zacharias' son. Perhaps this was what old Zacharias had been looking forward to so much. It was certainly clear that the son would be named after his father, of course. He would carry on the name, probably enter the temple service, be a great credit to his father, and to Elizabeth, too.

So, Sandor arrived on the day of blessing. There were a few others of the close neighbors there as well. Sandor was wondering if it was going to be frustrating for Zacharias, not being able to communicate well. But the celebration went along rather well, until the time came for the official naming. Then, when the name Zacharias was used, old Zacharias became agitated, shaking his head strenuously. They asked him what name he wanted, and he found a way to write. The name he wrote was John!

Sandor could feel a sense that the neighbors were beginning to think that more than Zacharias' speech had been affected that day, and there was an uncomfortable atmosphere in the room. Maybe this wasn't such a good idea, having so many people over today.

Then, all of a sudden, Zacharias smiled, and took a deep breath, and to the amazement of all, said, in a clear, strong voice: "His name is John!"

When Sandor thought back on it later, he realized that was when his life changed. He wasn't just a neighbor being nice to an old couple he really liked. He wasn't just a visitor at a friend's special event. He was a witness to the world changing from left to right, from old to new, from darkness to light.

The rest of the time Sandor was there that day he had listened with a sense of awe to Zacharias talk about his experience in the temple. He listened to Zacharias describe the great expectation he had for his son's life. His son was not just going to be a blessing to Zacharias and Elizabeth. He was not just going to be serving in the temple. He was going to get the way ready for Messiah to come!

The great promise was actually going to be fulfilled! God was taking action! He was stepping into their time! It was going to be soon! It was starting now. It had started that day at the naming of John. It had started, Sandor realized, earlier. It had started on a day when he went to the temple to worship, wondering who was serving. The fulfillment had started with an angel appearing to an old friend, in the temple, on a day that people would always remember. And he had been there!

2. The Visit

Esther had always enjoyed her visits to Elizabeth. Elizabeth and her husband, who served in the temple, lived close by. When Esther visited, the loss of her mother didn't weigh so much on her heart. Of course, it was a small town, but it was wonderful, Ester thought, how much there was to talk about that was happening right here.

Then there was the amazing change. Their conversation had so often been about Elizabeth's sadness about not having children, and particularly not having a son for her husband. Now since Elizabeth was pregnant, what a difference! Sadness had disappeared, and conversations were about preparations for her son (how could she be sure, Esther wondered).

Elizabeth talked about her husband's experience with the angel, but Esther wasn't so sure. Men! Well, honestly, Esther thought, she was really thinking about her brother who could come up with the most amazing stories about why something happened. They were usually designed to get him out of any blame for what otherwise would surely have been his fault. But, well, Elizabeth, after all those years, was pregnant.

They had agreed to get together again soon, and Esther was wondering how Elizabeth was feeling now that she was in her last trimester.

As Esther came, she had another surprise when she entered Elizabeth's home. There was already someone there. She was a young woman, surely not more than 17. Elizabeth introduced her as a distant niece, or something like that. It had been a few weeks since Esther had visited, but she hadn't expected quite so much of a change. She thought

12

she had seen Elizabeth excited and joyful before, but now she seemed absolutely jubilant. The young woman, Mary it turned out here name was, was quiet but when she talked she had a striking sense of confidence.

After they got settled, Elizabeth asked Mary, "Will you please be willing to let Esther in on the wonderful news you bring?" "Do you think she'll believe me?" Mary asked. Elizabeth answered, "I think it may be just what Esther needs. Yes, I think she will believe you more than she has me."

Esther started to say that she really believed Elizabeth, but Mary looked at her with a kind, thoughtful gaze that touched Esther deeply, and Esther stopped speaking in response.

Mary started to speak, quietly and vibrantly, "You see, I have talked to an angel. I'm sitting here quietly enjoying your company, I have travelled for several days to get here, but two weeks ago yesterday, at a few minutes after 10 in the morning, I was sitting behind my home in Nazareth, when an angel appeared and started talking to me." Mary paused to let her words sink in and then said, "May I continue?"

Esther took a deep breath, let it out, and said, "Ok, please go on, I'm as ready as I'll ever be."

"You see," Mary went on, "I'm engaged to a wonderful man. His name is Joseph. We've known each other for a few years. This isn't a sudden thing. It was about Joseph I was thinking, as I was sitting outside in the back. Suddenly, I wasn't alone. I saw someone walking toward me, just seeming to come from the air. He said I was highly favored and that the Lord was with me. As you can imagine, I haven't had a lot of people say that to me. Well, not any."

"I suppose I was starting to shake from fear and nerves, because then he told me not to be afraid. He said that I had found favor with God." Mary paused and then said, "Now, I should mention that I do spend time every day talking to the Lord. I talk to Him about my family, about Joseph, about what we want in our future together. I have even talked to Him about how frustrated we are waiting for His promises in His word to be fulfilled. It was as if the angel knew all that. He went on to say that I was going to have a baby, a son. He said I would name our son Jesus. And then ..., well, he said Jesus would be called great, the son of the Most High, and that God will give him King David's throne. He said Jesus will reign over the house of Jacob, and that his kingdom will never end."

"I suppose it was pretty brash of me to say anything to the angel, but at that point I really had trouble seeing how this was supposed to happen, so I spoke up and said that Joseph and I were just engaged. But the angel lifted my heart with wonder and joy when he told me it was the Holy Spirit and the power of the Most High that were going to make this happen. Then he said—take a deep breath again, Esther—he said our son would be called Holy, the Son of God."

Esther tried to say something, but she was finding it difficult to have any sounds come out. Elizabeth took her hand and said, "You see why I am filled with joy, Esther? Messiah is coming. The promises are being fulfilled. You are talking to the mother of the Messiah!"

"You mean the time is coming when you're going to..." Esther was spluttering a little.

"No," said Mary, "not sometime."

"You mean, ..."

Quietly Mary said, "Now."

3. A Sheep Story

Sam was trying, again, to remember why he was out on this cold, dark field with these smelly sheep. There had been his uncle's request to help him out. There had been his mother's smile when she said, "It'll be good for you." (How, exactly was that likely to be, he wondered.) There was, of course, some money he got. Didn't seem like a lot, but it helped.

It wasn't so much the smell—it wasn't as bad as when he started six months ago. Had the day crew been giving them baths? Probably just his nose not working as well, he thought. The real problem with sheep he decided was that they were so ornery. They made up their minds and they just wouldn't listen to reason. He remembered Mabel who seemed determined to walk off that cliff on the way to settling in for the night.

Sam remembered, too, the way his granny told him that was why God called His people His sheep. That didn't seem very nice. Well, it might apply to some people, he thought, but not to him—well, ok, to him, too, but at least not very often.

The night just seemed to go on forever for Sam. He found it excruciatingly boring. Dark and boring. Chilly and dark and boring. It wasn't even that he had a lot of responsibility. The chief shepherd was the one in charge. He seemed to like the outdoor life. He made sure each sheep was ok each night. If there were any injuries, he made sure they were taken care of. Sam would have preferred a little action in the night. It was hard to stay awake. If perhaps a visitor would stop by to tell stories, now that, Sam thought would be a great break from the monotony.

Sam was just wondering who he would pick to come and break the monotony (not Zeke, his stories only made sense to Zeke), when suddenly, there was a light so brilliant that it hurt his eyes. He stumbled backward and fell down. As he was struggling to see again, he realized there was someone talking to him and the other shepherds. Maybe he had wished too much for someone to come and tell stories, but this was way beyond that—this was very scary.

The voice was telling them not to be afraid. Well, more than a voice. It was a person. But not like any person Sam had ever seen. This was a person that was surrounded by light the way Sam was surrounded by air. This person of light was saying that there was good news about something that was a wonderful joy intended for all people.

Something was happening in the town, Bethlehem. Something about a Savior. (That was Messiah, Sam thought. But that was supposed to be way in the future some time, not now. Not today. Not in the middle of the night.) A Savior that was born. Sam struggled with this thought. He was pretty sure Messiah was coming with might and power. He was coming by breaking into the world to let everyone know God was in charge. And He was coming to make everything right again, all the things that were problems, all the frustrations, all the suffering. How could a baby do all that?! Wait! Had he heard it right? The baby was Messiah, the Christ, the Lord in person?

Sam was just beginning to puzzle through what he had heard, when zap! There was even more light! The whole hillside was covered with these strange people of light. Without any pause of introduction or explanation, they burst into wonderful, stupendous singing, glorifying God. Wait until the Rabbi at the synagogue hears about this, thought Sam! He had never heard any music like this before. Glorious, joyous, uplifting, exciting. It was nourishing, giving him a new strength, not just to be awake in the middle of this night, but to want to do something. He didn't think of himself as a singer, but he sure wished he could join in with this group and sing like that! But it wasn't just glory to God they were singing. It was about how God loved and cared about people, especially the people who wanted God to come and keep His promises.

Then click! They were all gone. Sam felt like his ears had been turned off, it was so quiet. He felt blind, it was so dark. Then he could hear the chief shepherd say, "The angels told us how to find Messiah in a manger in Bethlehem. Come on! Let's go!"

The nourishment and energy Sam had taken in from the singing must have been very strong, because Sam didn't hesitate. He and all the shepherds followed the chief shepherd across the hills to Bethlehem. Sam expected the town to be in an uproar, but it was dark and quiet as if nothing had happened. Where would they find a baby in a place where there was a hay manger for animals?

The shepherds hurried through town, looking for some light, some activity in the night. Then one of the shepherds said, "The inn! I'll bet there are animals there, out back." So, they headed to the inn, and behind it, where there were some animals kept, sure enough, they spotted a faint light. It was an oil lamp. There was a man holding a young woman. And a baby was laying there, wrapped in cloths, in the manger for the animals. The couple looked up as the shepherds clattered through the silent night and came to a sudden halt in front of the young family.

"Angels, we saw!" "Glorious music!" "Promised Savior!" Words tumbled out of one after another of the shepherds, too loudly for the peaceful scene in front of them. But, Sam was thinking, this didn't look glorious. This didn't look like a Lord coming to fix the world. Where were the other people celebrating the fulfillment?

17

Then Sam watched the young woman and saw how her look of surprise turned to an amazingly beautiful look of peace and total satisfaction, as if everything was the way it was supposed to be. After the shepherds finished exploding with their spluttering words of wonder, explanation, and awe, the man said, "Thank you. We wondered if anyone would know. So this is how it is beginning. Glory be to God! Thank you for letting us know of God's messengers. And I suppose you are now God's messengers, too. The Lord be with you."

The chief shepherd then said something polite, like thank you for letting us come, and we'll let you get back to your peaceful night. Sam was never really sure. But Sam remembered the next part of the evening all his life. The shepherds (who now seemed unaware of the meaning of quiet) went through the town. Each one seemed to know who they wanted to find. They spread out, being anything but quiet—singing, laughing, celebrating. And they found people and made enough racket to wake them up, telling them their version of the wonder and glory and joy they had seen and heard.

Sam suddenly thought of his Granny. She had to know this! He went through the dark and quiet streets, not caring that there was a song not only in his heart but coming out of his mouth into the night silence. He was going to tell Granny that all those stories she had told him were real, not just for someday, but for now, for today. He was going to tell her about the angels. (Is that who they were! Amazing!) And he was going to tell her about the couple in the stable and the Baby. The Baby, who was the One she was waiting for.

Just before knocking on her door to share the good news, Sam paused to wonder. Would he ever see the baby again? What was going to change? Would he ever see the baby when he was grown up? Whatever else happened he knew his life had changed. OK, Granny, he thought, get ready for a surprise!

4. Anna's Reason

Everybody knew Anna. She had been faithfully coming to the temple each day for as long as anyone could remember.

She didn't come to the temple to meet and greet people. She didn't come as a social event in her senior years. She came to serve God. That was it. Every day, every night she gave service to God with fasting and praying. Sometimes it sounded like she was grieving with God, sometimes laughing with God, as if there was a private joke they enjoyed. But today she was praising God.

Sena was a widow as was Anna. Though Sena was a lot younger, she enjoyed being with Anna. She, too, loved coming to the temple to be with God, to talk to God, to lean on God's love and grace when times were difficult. They had been difficult when her husband died. Then her children grew up and moved on to lives of their own. She came into the temple now and saw Anna praising God. When Sena came close, Anna turned to her and said, "Sena! Have you heard? He's come!"

"No", Sena said, "I just got here. Who's come?"

In answer, Anna took Sena by the arm and led her to Simeon. Sena knew Simeon as a legend there in the temple. He had been coming to the temple for years, also. Whenever anyone asked him how he was, he always said the same thing, "Waiting." But now he looked different.

"Simeon!", said Anna, "Tell Sena!"

"He's come!" said Simeon, "And I'm going home."

"Who's come?" asked Sena, with excitement growing.

"There", Simeon said, pointing, "there He is. That young couple is carrying Him."

"The baby?"

"Yes! Remember I told you the Lord showed me that I could live to see Messiah come. And when I came this morning, the Lord opened my eyes to recognize Him. That's Jesus, with His mother Mary and Joseph her husband. Right. I didn't know I was waiting for a baby. But now it's clear. Messiah has come. The Lord has fulfilled His promise to me and His promise to us."

"How…?"

"It wasn't what I expected either. The Lord hasn't made everything clear to me, but that Child is going to live through some very difficult and dark days. There will be sorrow and grief as well as joy and satisfaction. In the end, God will fulfill His promise to us, to cleanse us from all evil and sin, and to bring us to Him forever."

"Tell her about the Gentiles," Anna encouraged.

"Right. The Lord has shown me that He will be Messiah not just for us, but for all people. He will bring His eternal light to the Gentiles as well."

"But how can there be sorrow and grief, Simeon?"

"Sena, I think the difference is that some people are considering success to be seeking the Lord. And some people are just seeking success, by using the Lord and His promises. I think there is going to be a collision of the two."

Anna asked, "How did the parents take what you said?"

21

"They took it pretty well. I think they are walking very closely with the Lord and have come to the point of expecting the Lord to open each day with His own plans in His good will—whether they exactly understand it or not."

"And you, Simeon, are you ready to leave?"

"Yes, Anna, the Lord has satisfied my heart completely. We have been waiting for this moment for thousands of years, and I am greatly privileged to have seen the Light from the Lord begin to shine through Messiah Who has finally come. I have been put here to wait. To wait for this moment. Others will see the Fulfillment unfold. My time has come to an end, and I rejoice to go home to the Lord."

As Anna and Sena watched, Simeon was still smiling as he walked out of the temple for the last time.

Sena said, "Let me come and praise our Lord with you, Anna." "Yes, Sena," Anna replied, "the Lord has given us reason to praise."

After they spent some time in worship and praise Anna said, "Sena, I know now, that my time for serving with worship and praise is coming to an end, also. I have seen the Fulfillment start. You are going to see a lot more of that Child in your life. And…" then Anna paused as if listening, "and I think…, yes, through sorrow and joy, you will have great reason to come and praise. I think you are going to be my replacement."

5. Strange Gifts

Ari had lived in Bethlehem for quite a while. He was satisfied with being in the small town with his little shop. A few times a year, though, he liked to go up to Jerusalem. It was a different feeling to be in the city with its busyness, with people coming back home from the distant places where they now lived, and, yes, even with its traffic problems and crowded space.

He usually stayed with his cousin Rafi and Rafi's wife, Nina. This trip was not for a festival. He was just doing some shopping and enjoying the capitol. It was the third day he was there that Nina came home from the market and called for Rafi and Ari to come hear the news.

"Visitors!" she said.

"Another trade caravan?" asked Rafi.

"No. These are real visitors! They look like a royal delegation the way they're dressed. Even their camels look a little snooty, they way they are decked out with amazing colors. Apparently, they've come to see Herod."

"Be interesting to hear what they're here for. You still have that contact in the palace, Rafi?" asked Ari.

"Yes," Rafi said, "I'll go see what I can find out."

It was an hour later that Rafi came back. He didn't look particularly pleased. "What is it, Rafi?" Nina asked.

"Well, I found out why the fancy visitors have come. They saw Herod. And if you can believe it, they asked Herod where the One is that has been born, King of the Jews."

"They said that to Herod?" Nina and Ari asked together. "That doesn't sound good."

"That's what they asked," said Rafi. "My friend says that first Herod's face turned a nasty shade of purple. Then he calmed down and became ever so polite. He told them he would check on it and get back to them. He's supposed to see them tomorrow."

"Where are these people from to come to Herod (he who is totally in charge!) and say that?" Ari asked. "It appears," Rafi said, "that they are from a country east of here, on the other side of the desert. They don't appear to care who Herod is or how he feels about anything."

"Not good!" Nina muttered.

It was the next day when Rafi came with news for the others. "Well, they met with Herod again. And Herod told them—are you ready for this, Ari?—the experts in the palace have said the promised King of Israel is the Messiah and He is supposed to be born in your town, Bethlehem. What's been happening in Bethlehem that you haven't told us?"

"I don't think I have been keeping anything back, Rafi. I think I mentioned, a little over a year ago I think it was, that there were some shepherds that had a pretty wild story of seeing angels and something about the hotel stable. I think there might have been a baby mentioned now that I remember. But I don't remember anything about a King."

"OK. I suppose we'll have to wait and see what happens," said Rafi. "Herod, my friend says, sent the visitors off to see what they could find. Apparently, they have come to worship this new King. They are supposed to come back and tell Herod, so he can go and worship, too."

"Like that would ever happen!" exclaimed Nina. "Not so loud," cautioned Rafi, "you never know who might be from the palace listening."

"The thing is, Ari," said Rafi, "it might be a good idea for you to head back home, and just keep an eye on what happens." "Yes, I can see that," said Ari. "When Herod sniffs any kind of opposition to his being 'totally in charge' it isn't pretty. I'll head back today."

When Ari got home, he asked his wife, Zibiah, if anything happened while he was gone. "You mean the group with the camels, I suppose. Got here yesterday. They've been asking around about a baby. We've had quite a few in the last year or so. What's going on, anyway?"

Ari explained what had happened with the visitors and their interview with Herod. "That doesn't sound good," Zibiah said. "See, that's what Rafi and his wife and I said, too," agreed Ari. "Well I'm getting back to the shop. Let me know if you hear anything."

By evening, Zibiah had news. "You know that young couple that took the little house old Zack had? Out at the edge of town? Apparently, that's where they ended up, these visitors. Joseph, I think his name is. Not sure about her name."

It wasn't until noon the following day that Ari, coming home, found Zibiah bubbling with more news. "You'll never guess what those strange people did when they visited that young couple, Ari," Zibiah said. "OK, spill it, what now?" said Ari. "They brought presents for the baby!" "Well, … I suppose … you mean they came all that way to bring some baby things?" said Ari.

25

"No! Not baby things. Gold! And frankincense and myrrh! And they fell down before the little baby and actually worshiped Him."

"Are you telling me," asked Ari, "those were the gifts they brought?" "Yes, what do you think of that!" she responded.

"Well, gold I suppose is a blessing for a young couple getting started, although a little extreme as a present. But frankincense is … what, for sacrifices in the temple, right? And myrrh, that's what's used for burials. Those are really pretty strange gifts."

"That's what I thought," said Zibiah. "What is the world coming to!"

Ari felt so puzzled, that he decided to go out on his afternoon off and see what he could find out. As he was walking through town, he met the young husband, Joseph, and couldn't help asking, "I understand you've had visitors?"

Joseph smiled, "I guess word travels pretty fast in any small town. Yes, we have indeed. I'll tell you what, why don't you and your wife come by later this afternoon. We'll enjoy a visit with you."

Ari could hardly wait to get home and tell Zibiah. When they had waited a respectful hour, they hurried over to visit the young couple.

Joseph welcomed them to the little home, and introduced them to his wife, Mary, and their, not quite so little anymore, son, Jesus. Ari found Joseph and Mary to be two of the nicest and most humble people he had ever met and listened to Joseph describe the amazing visit they had received. Then Joseph even showed them the gifts which the visitors had brought for Jesus.

Ari asked, "Do you know why they brought these particular gifts?" "Not exactly," Joseph said, "but we are sure it will become clear. God has been guiding us this far, and I'm sure He will let us know."

After their visit, Ari and Zibiah talked about how impressed they were with meeting Joseph and Mary, and their son, who apparently had a future that was going to be a blessing not only for Him, but for their nation as well. They didn't understand how this was fulfilling God's promises, but they looked forward to seeing what was going to happen. It had been an awesome experience for both of them. They felt like God had touched them personally with a great blessing.

On the way back home, Ari and Zibiah saw a foreign servant buying some things in town. They asked if he was with the visitors that had come. "Yes," the servant replied, "we have come a long way, and now we must quickly return." "So soon?" asked Ari. "Yes. The One Who has spoken to send us here has spoken again, and we must leave."

It wasn't until the next day, that Ari learned from one of his customers that one of Herod's spies had been asking about the visitors that had come. Ari went home and told his wife, "I think there is trouble coming. Herod has been snooping around asking about the visitors that were supposed to come back and report to him."

Zibiah said, "That doesn't sound good at all. You need to go find Joseph and Mary and let them know that Herod is going to do something." Ari went out as quickly as he could to give a word of warning.

He came back a few minutes later, and Zibiah asked, "Have you found them and warned them?" "Well, not exactly," said Ari. "What do you mean?" asked Zibiah. "I went to their house to tell them," said Ari, "but…they're gone!"

6. The Student's Parents

Melech got up early as usual. As he got ready to walk to the temple for the day's discussions, he thought about how satisfied he was. He had been a good student growing up. He remembered how surprised his parents were when he had told them he wanted to be a teacher.

He had needed help from his uncle, Lem, of course, to be able to finance his education. But it had been worth it. Now these many years later he looked back on the students he had taught. Some had been difficult. Some were just distracted most of the time—sports, girls, military training and such things. But there had been some good students, too.

Now that he had been selected to participate in the Sanhedrin, he was especially satisfied. An honor, yes, it truly was to sit with other teachers of note and discuss important questions in God's law—His will revealed in His word and in the writings of the famous scholars.

Today's discussion would be different and rather interesting, since they would be outside their normal meeting chambers. They would be in the part of the temple available to those who wanted to hear what was discussed and possibly even ask a question or two. Yes, Melech thought, it should be interesting today.

It wasn't exactly showing off how much they knew, discussing the law of God in public. Although possibly some of the Sanhedrin members did rather enjoy that. No, it really was a chance to stretch the imagination and understanding of those who came to hear. That's the way Melech looked at it.

Those that came to hear were usually men with some experience in thinking about the law. Some were teachers from outlying areas. Some had wanted to be teachers and had needed to go into some other field of work. There were some of the general public, possibly agricultural workers, for whom it was like listening to those from another world. Very few children, of course. They just weren't interested.

So out Melech went with the others of the Sanhedrin to see who showed up this morning and to enjoy discussing the topic of the day. As they settled in and began their discussion, (today the topic was God's love for His people), Melech looked around to see what kind of group they had attracted. He was surprised to see that there was a young person there. A young man of about twelve, he appeared. Rather unusual!

Sholum was holding forth in his exposition of the topic in his usual rather pedantic fashion. Melech was surprised to see that the young man was fully attentive and rather engrossed with the presentation. After a while Sholum came to a pause and asked if there were any questions, which at this point was mostly just polite, since he didn't expect to get any.

To their surprise there was a question, and it was the young man that Melech had noticed that asked it. He said, "Sir, you have described well the love of God. Do you enjoy it?"

Now Sholum had spoken for many years on topics in the law, and possibly because of his rather dry treatment of his subjects, he had not had many questions. Melech noticed a certain frustration on Sholum's face. He did not appear to appreciate the question he had received. Sholum seemed to be thinking, "Described it well?! Why I should think so!"

He said to the young man, "I know that in your young years you are beginning to enjoy many things. I think you will come to understand when you are older that God's love is

29

something more to comprehend and recognize than it is something to enjoy."

Sholum was about to go on to his next point, when, almost casually, the young man said, "So you don't enjoy it. I'm sorry to hear that."

Melech had a small sense of satisfaction at the discomfiture that Sholum displayed as he jumped rather hastily into his next area of discussion. The discussion that followed was intriguing to Melech, and the rest of the day passed without incident. Melech didn't give much thought to the young man again that day.

The next day, however, when the august group of teachers gathered for their second day of public discussions, Melech noticed to his amazement that the young man had returned. This time he asked the presenter several questions and showed real intellect and insight for someone so young. After one of the young man's comments, Sholum asked him a question. The question required a familiarity of several points of God's will and their relationship to each other. Melech thought Sholum was probably trying to put this young man in his place.

To Melech's amazement (and certainly Sholum's) the young man gave an answer that was not only knowledgeable but insightful and rather intriguing. Melech enjoyed the interchange and noticed that Sholum didn't try that again.

After the second day's discussions, Melech and Sholum discussed the young man. "What school of training, do you suppose, he comes from?" Melech asked. Sholum said, "He has to be with a rabbi in Jerusalem, doesn't he?"

"Yes, I agree," said Melech, "but he doesn't have the right accent somehow. I wonder where he does come from. We may not ever find out, I suppose. I wish I had him as a

30

student. He would be a pleasure to teach. He's got quite a future ahead of him. I'd like to see how he develops a few years from now."

But the next day, the last of the public discussions of the Sanhedrin for this term, the young man was back, still looking very interested. Melech was just thinking that he had never seen any man with him, and wondered where his father was, when a young couple came up and exclaimed, "Jesus! Where have you been? We've been looking all over for you! Why have you done this to us?"

The young man just seemed rather surprised. He hugged the two, obviously his parents, and appeared glad to see them. But he said, "Didn't you know I had to be in my Father's house?"

Melech watched them walk away, puzzled by what had happened. It was later, when he and Sholum were discussing the day's events, that the subject of the young man came up. "Very strange, his parents showing up like that," said Sholum. "We probably should have been concerned earlier, not seeing anyone with him," said Melech.

Sholum stood for a moment, with a puzzled look on his face. Then he started, "What was that about his parents not knowing where he was. … Then he said they should have known he was in his father's house? … Of course, God is indeed our father." While Melech was walking away, he heard Sholum going on to himself, "So, surely he meant… Didn't he?"

7. A Fisherman's Change

Andy and Naty had made the trip from Galilee to Jerusalem last week. It had seemed a long trip, walking through the plains and then up into the mountains. They had talked about the idea that somebody ought to smooth out this path to make this trip easier. Enough people travel to Jerusalem, after all.

Now they had made the purchases for which they had come. They had taken time to go to the temple. Since they had started making the trip for supplies and worship time, they had seen some grand changes that Herod had made in the temple area. "What do you think, Andy," Naty had asked, "is it Herod's fire insurance, is he really trying to get in good with the Lord?" "Why Naty," Andy answered, "how could you be so pessimistic about our great leader?" But the sarcasm was clearly evident on Andy's face when he said it.

That morning they heard about a strange desert hermit that had suddenly appeared near the Jordan River, down the east side of the mountain from Jerusalem. Apparently, his name was John, although some people were calling him the Baptizer. He was preaching a message of a New Beginning to the crowds of people that were coming from all over the country to hear him.

"Come on, Naty," Andy said, "let's go down to see what he has to say." "Andy, you realize that means going down the mountain and coming up again before heading home, you think it's that interesting?" Naty replied.

"Yes, this might be important. And if nothing else, it will be quite different from thinking about fishing all the time," Andy said. It took a little encouragement, but the two of them left their animals and purchases with a friend in Jerusalem and headed down the mountain to see what the strange desert man had to say.

They were amazed when they got close. There had been a few times when they thought it might be hard to find this John, but as they got to the bottom of the mountain, they saw large crowds of people heading for the river and realized that they had found what they were looking for.

They asked one of the men in the crowd what the attraction was. "Oh, I've come several days," he said. "At first, I was put off by what this John looks like and his somewhat harsh words. But now I have come to believe that God has sent him to us to really bless us. Come and see what you think."

As they got close enough to hear John, they could tell what the man meant. John was practically shouting at the people telling them it was time for them to repent of the things they had done wrong. Someone was coming Who expected some pretty big changes. John was particularly strident in his message to some of the Jewish leaders who had made the trip from Jerusalem. Andy and Naty were amazed at the lack of respect John showed. John seemed to think they were especially in need of change and repentance.

John's message seemed to be that people needed to make preparations. Changes needed to be made. Like a king coming to the distant parts of his kingdom, the Lord was coming. In the old days, the people got the roads ready and the town cleaned up and ready for the king's coming. Now, John was telling people they needed to clean up themselves and their attitudes and their actions because they wanted to be ready to receive the Lord without being embarrassed when He came.

One of the changes John called for seemed to particularly incense the leaders. He told them to stop being so arrogant about being "children of Abraham" and wait for the Lord's coming with humility and repentance.

Andy murmured to Naty that he thought they deserved those words. He had always thought there were some of the leaders who considered themselves way above everyone else. Then Andy started thinking about some of the things he had said to others in the fishing business they had, to some customers, and even to Naty, and he found himself blushing.

After listening for a while Andy was impressed and moved and Naty was blessed, too. The question that came into Andy's mind was finally asked by someone else—"What is this new life, this readiness, going to look like?"

John responded that those people who were blessed with a lot should share with those who are in need. (Andy found himself nodding in agreement and thinking about himself.) John said that tax collectors should only collect what they had been assigned to collect without padding their bills with incredible amounts which they kept for themselves. (This time Andy was close to a cheer or an "Amen!") John told soldiers to be content with their wages. He seemed to be telling everyone that it was really all right to be satisfied with what they had without living to get more and more. (Andy found himself taking that in more quietly, feeling like John was talking to him.)

The day came to a close in time to head back up the mountain to Jerusalem. On the way Andy found himself mulling over what he had heard. This was more than just a new thought, more than just news to share with the people at home. John had touched him personally. He talked to Naty and said, "So, the prophecies are really being fulfilled. I guess I hadn't thought it would look like this, though." "Yes," Naty said, "I know what you mean. I used to think that there was going to be some flash of lightening, beautiful music,

34

and everyone happy. But I can see what John means about preparation being necessary." "Yes," Andy said, "so can I." They were quiet then for a long time.

When they got to Jerusalem and gathered their belongings, Naty said, "So, we'll leave tomorrow morning for home?"

Andy took a moment, drew a deep breath, and said, "No, Naty. There are going to be some changes. There is something happening that is truly great. When John talked about not being worthy of being a slave for the Lord that is coming, God touched me."

"I know this is difficult, but I believe that God is calling me. I've never felt like this before, Naty. I need you to help me. You need to take the supplies home."

"What!" came from Naty.

"Yes," said Andy with enthusiasm and certainty rising in his voice. "I need you to take the supplies home. I'm going back."

"Going back! It's going to get dark soon. You can't go down the mountain now!"

"There's a full moon. I'll be fine. I'm going back and find John. There are things John talked about … I need to know more. Baptism with the Holy Spirit. The Lord coming. Yes, I'm going to go back. You go home and tell my brother what you've seen and heard. Tell him what I've said. Tell him … I'm going to find the Lord, Naty."

As he left the amazed Naty and headed back, Andy shouted, "Tell my brother! I'm going to find the Lord! Tell Peter!"

8. Next in Line

Asher and Mina had agreed to come and hear the desert prophet after their neighbor, Shaya, had told them his experience. Shaya told them that this prophet made a lot more sense than the somewhat boring leaders they had heard in their local synagogue. For Shaya it had been a life-changing experience, he had said. It was a new beginning. And Asher and Mina wanted that kind of blessing in their lives.

So, they agreed to let Shaya take them down the mountain into the Jordan valley where the prophet was preaching to the people who came from all parts of the country.

There were indeed large crowds of people who had come to hear this desert prophet. Listening to him, Asher and Mina could understand why Shaya had been touched and brought to a change in his life. The prophet was straightforward and honest, showing the way that people lived in selfishness and fear, ignoring God and His will. At the same time, he pictured a new life here and now with an attitude of repentance and commitment to God and his will.

Shaya described to Asher and Mina what that had meant to him. He had stopped making decisions based on what he thought was best for him and listened to God's encouragement to care about other people.

The Prophet, his name was John, Shaya told them, was fearless in his attitude toward those in authority. He gave them the same message of repent from self-centered living and begin anew. For Asher and Mina it was a refreshing eye-opening experience.

"Well," said Asher, "I guess the question is do we want ..."
"Oh, Asher," Mina broke in, "stop being so analytical. Of
course we want this. We need to stop thinking only about
ourselves and think about God's will for us. We need to be
baptized and begin a new life together, right?" "Yes," Asher
said. "That is exactly what we need."

"Shaya, what do we do next?"

"Wait a few moments until John is finished, and he will ask if
anyone wants to be baptized in repentance and into a new
life. Then a line will form of people waiting to be baptized
and you just get in line."

So, Asher and Mina got into the line that started to form a
few minutes later. There were a lot of people who came into
the line. There wasn't any pushing and shoving the way
there sometimes was when people line up to wait. Everyone
seemed satisfied that they were in a group of people like
themselves who wanted God's blessing in a new way.

Mina started to talk to the folks behind them in line. It turned
out they were a husband and wife who farmed in the valley,
a little farther north. Then she turned to the man in front of
them. He seemed a quiet sort of man, somewhat alone in
the crowd.

He asked them why they had gotten in line, and Asher
explained their desire to change from focusing only on
themselves to a new beginning that involved listening to
what God wanted. Asher also explained Shaya's experience
and how he had brought them to John because it had meant
so much to him to break with his past and start anew.

It was easy to talk to the man, he was sympathetic and a
good listener. Asher told him about the difficulties they
faced. It seemed like everyone in the business world was
focused on what they could get for themselves. God didn't

seem to fit into their lives, except in some token, perfunctory way with completing the right ceremony at the right time. God's word and faithful living didn't seem to be a part of the lives of most people Asher and Mina knew. And Asher admitted that it was easy to stray into the idea that money and power were the most important things in life.

Asher found himself sharing his dreams of a new life that involved running his business at the edge of Jerusalem in a way that showed that God came first in his life and that he cared about other people before himself. He talked about his idea to have not just food and drink available to his customers, but also maybe a room upstairs where they could have celebrations.

As they were getting closer to the front of the line, Mina said, "We've been talking about ourselves a lot. Why have you come here?"

"Well, like you," the man said, "I have come to make a commitment, to start this part of my life in a new way. I'm making some changes, also. In fact, my father asked me to come."

"Is your father here, too, then?" asked Mina.

"You probably won't see him," the man said. And then as if to himself, he murmured, "but you might hear him, I suppose."

"Are you from a large family," Mina asked, which Asher, somewhat disconcerted, thought was a little forward. "That's all right," said the man, sensing Asher's discomfort. "No, I'm an only son."

"Do you have plans for after you are baptized?" Mina went on. The man smiled and said, "Yes, I'm going to be traveling. I have a lot of people to see. But first I plan to spend some time getting focused by going into the desert."

Asher was thinking that that plan didn't sound like a very practical plan for making a living, but he was too polite to say anything.

"You see," the man went on, "I have an assignment from my father. He'll be providing for me. Thank you for caring." Asher felt a little strange that his thought was being answered, but found himself encouraged just sharing with this man who happened to be in front of them in line.

"Oh, I think it's my turn," the man said. As Asher and Mina watched he walked out into the water to John, and then a strange thing happened. Instead of the usual words from John, the baptism, and moving along to the next person, John started talking to this man. They talked for a minute together, then John bowed his head briefly and then looked up before baptizing this man.

It was then that it happened. It was hard for Asher and Mina to take it all in. There was a sudden bright light that came from overhead. The very sky itself seemed to tear open to let in this overwhelmingly bright light. And something, it might have been a dove they thought, came flying down from the opening in the sky. Then there was a sound. Loud, but not shouting. Just loud enough for everyone, maybe for a long way, to hear. Something, Asher thought later, about "my beloved son."

It seemed to Mina and Asher as if the world were standing still, as if waiting for something. It was hard to tell for them, it might have been a few minutes or just an instant. Then the moment broke, and the world seemed to start up again. "Wow," said Asher, "this is a new beginning! Mina, who do you suppose that man is?"

"Yes," Mina said, as they headed toward John in the water, "did you hear that?" Just then the man was on his way to shore, and he leaned toward them in passing and said, "My name's Jesus. And the upper room's a good idea."

9. His Smile

Cana. It wasn't very far from Nazareth. In Cana, if you stood in the right place, you could see part of Nazareth. Cana is where Mary had been coming to help her cousin Besel with the plans for the wedding.

Besel's son was getting married, and she appreciated Mary's calm, thoughtful, and caring help as she went through the weeks and months of preparing for the big event. When Besel felt frazzled, she would talk to Mary and things seemed possible and even well-ordered.

Invitations had been sent out, and Besel felt confident that friends and family were going to come. The wedding couple would be properly honored. Of course, Mary was going to be there. So, it was only reasonable to invite her son, Jesus. Admittedly it was a little disconcerting that apparently Jesus was teaching a group of men who followed him and stayed with him. It had been just a few days before the wedding that they had all come up to Nazareth, but the invitation had to be expanded to include them as well. Besel had a fleeting thought wondering if the supplies would hold out, but some other planning need came up, and the thought disappeared.

The great event was planned for a beautiful yard next to the house. Everything had been set up well. All the invited guests had come (rather amazing really), and everything seemed to be going well.

The disciples who were with Jesus were still getting used to being disciples and having a wonderful rabbi who led them and taught them. It did seem a little strange to them that their rabbi seemed to enjoy life more than other rabbis they had seen. Others seemed to be serious teachers who only focused on learning and keeping the right rules and

41

procedures. Jesus, and certainly today the disciples as well, seemed to be enjoying life and in particular this wedding celebration.

Then, Mary came to their table and leaning over to Jesus told him that she had just found out from Besel that the supply of wine was getting dangerously low. She didn't have to tell him that the situation could be disastrous for the newly married couple for years to come ("remember, those are the ones that didn't have enough wine!").

Mary had depended on Jesus even more after Joseph died. Jesus appreciated the way that Mary came to him. He was glad to be able to help her for a little while longer. He let her know that he liked her coming to him and that he would take care of the situation. He also let her know that his time to be openly in the light of public scrutiny with wonder and awe had not yet come.

Mary didn't have a clue what Jesus was going to do, but she knew he wouldn't fail her. So, she went over to the wedding staff and told them to expect Jesus to contact them. She told them to do what he asked them even if they didn't understand why.

A few minutes after Mary had gone, Jesus called to Phineas their table waiter and asked where the purification water containers were. Phineas took him over by the house and showed him the six large stone containers. They were empty at the moment. Jesus asked Phineas, "Can you fill them with water?" Phineas answered, "Yes, if you would like me to." Jesus said, "Yes, please fill them."

After Phineas and others in the wedding service staff had filled all of the jars with water, Phineas came to Jesus and said, "The jars are all full of water now, sir." Phineas didn't say what he was thinking, but his thoughts were full of wondering why they had just put all that water in the jars.

The need, of course, was more wine. Phineas and the rest of the staff were getting a little nervous, because if the wine ran out, it wasn't just the couple that would be tarred with the memory in the minds of people, but also the wedding staff.

Jesus didn't seem worried or perturbed. He just said to Phineas, "Is there a wedding steward in charge?" Phineas said, with a little feeling of puzzlement, "Yes, it's old Motta, sir." "Good," said Jesus, "draw out some of the water and take it to him to taste." Jesus turned back to his disciples and they continued their conversation while Phineas, even more puzzled, went off to draw out some water.

Phineas had been doing weddings for some years, but this was a first. Taste the water. Hmmm. What would Motta say, he wondered. Should he back up after he handed Motta the water? Well, here goes, he thought.

Phineas came to Motta with the drawn water and started his hastily prepared spiel, "Motta, sir, we seem to have run out of the wine," and as Motta's face started to change color he hastened on, "but we've come across this and wonder if you would be willing to taste it." Phineas held his breath while Motta, with an expression between worry and puzzlement, slowly reached out to take the sample.

Motta tasted the sample and his face suddenly changed to an expression of wonder and surprise. "Have you tasted this?" he asked Phineas. "Oh, no sir," said Phineas. "Taste it!" So Phineas tasted it, too. "Wow, that's pretty good!" exclaimed Phineas. "Pretty good!" said Motta, "that's the best wine I've ever tasted at any wedding I've managed! And I've managed quite a few weddings!" "Where did they get this? … No, you wouldn't know, of course. … I need to talk to the groom. … Amazing! … In all my days."

Phineas started to say, "I suppose then it's all right …", as Motta was walking away, but then gave up. He went to

Yitzhak and told him to serve the guests from the water jars. Yitzhak started to ask, "But, why …" when Phineas said, "Don't ask. Take my word for it, they will enjoy it."

As Yitzhak went off, Phineas found himself muttering, "Wouldn't know … Of course I know! … I just don't know, well, how …" He was also thinking, These guests are never going to drink all that wine. The couple is going to have quite a wedding present. People will be asking them, "Do you still have any of that outstanding wine from your wedding left over?" They are going to be one popular couple.

Then Phineas looked over at the table where Jesus and his disciples were. They were just being served some of the new wine. He saw the disciples taste it—and saw their look of amazement on their faces. While Phineas was wondering what exactly had happened, suddenly, Jesus looked up, looked directly at Phineas, and smiled.

Phineas saw Jesus smile at him and thought his heart would stop.

Then with a feeling of great joy and satisfaction, he realized he was going to remember that smile for the rest of his life.

10. Somebody ought to ...

Meshel had been coming to Jerusalem for Passover every few years since they had moved to the outskirts of Rome. But this would be the first time for his seventeen-year-old son, Yuda.

Although this was a new experience for Yuda, he had prepared for the event. He had talked to their rabbi and listened carefully to his description of the Holy City of Jerusalem and what he should expect. Yuda had talked to a couple of others in their synagogue at home asking about their experiences in visiting Jerusalem. Now he figured he knew everything he needed to know.

So far, it had been a peaceful trip. It was a good voyage across the sea. They were staying with some distant relative here in the city. At home, Yuda enjoyed the food his mother prepared, but he was really enjoying the wonderful variety of foods here. They had stopped at several food booths, and Yuda had a few suggestions he was going to bring home to his mother.

Today was the high point of the trip. They had come to the temple itself. It stood majestically on a hill. The descriptions Yuda had heard didn't match the actual experience of being here and seeing this central focus of Jewish worship. Yuda's father had seen to it that Yuda had been brought up faithfully. He knew the history of his people and God's gracious choosing of them as His own people. He was familiar with the ceremonies and the law expressing the covenantal relationship God had with His people. He felt ready for the experience of going into the temple and making a sacrifice. It was going to be a great event in his life.

Meshel had told his son that they could only afford a small sacrifice, a pair of doves. That had seemed strange to Yuda, but he was sure it was going to be terrific, anyway. He knew they had been saving for a while for this trip, but he wondered why the costs were so high. He had some ideas about how to fix that problem, but he hadn't quite shared them with his father.

Now that they were approaching the wonderful and beautiful temple, Yuda asked his father, "Where do we get the sacrifice, Dad? There are some booths with doves over there. They look pretty good." His father had replied that they would have to wait until they got inside the temple itself, so they continued up the hill and into the temple.

Even before they went in, they could see it was a very busy area. There were a lot of people coming into the temple, but there were a lot of people sitting at booths inside the temple also. Yuda asked his father, "Dad, who are all these people?" "These," Meshel answered, "are the people who sell sacrifice animals that will be approved by the authorities for use in the temple." "Oh," replied Yuda trying to see the difference in the animals. "Why are those people there with all the money stacked up?" "Those," Meshel explained, "are the money changers that accept money from people coming from all over the world and give money that is acceptable in the temple to pay our yearly temple tax and to buy animals to sacrifice."

"That's pretty nice of them," said Yuda. "Well..." Meshel said, "they do charge a fee for that service." "How much?" Yuda asked. "Let's see. It's $7.50 for changing up to $45, and then another $7.50 for every $45 above that." "WHAT!?" was the gurgled shout that came from Yuda. "Dad, that's ..." Meshel could see the wheels turning in Yuda. "That's 16%!" Meshel felt thankful for his son's grasp of math and his skill in figuring. "Yes, I suppose so," he said.

Just then one of the money changers recognized Meshel and said, "Meshel, you're back! How are you?" Meshel returned the greeting and explained that his son was having trouble accepting the fees involved in changing money. "Yuda this is Lemel, he's been here for … how many years, Lemel?" "It's been twenty-two years now, Meshel." Lemel turned to Yuda and said, "You see there are some serious costs involved in being here. It's a business."

Meshel asked, "But you're doing all right, Lemel, yes?" "Yes Meshel, it's true, I'm glad to be here. I'm not open yet, but if you wait a little, I'll be open." "Sure," said Meshel. Yuda said he would look around for a few minutes.

Yuda came back just as Lemel was getting ready to open. "Dad!" "Yes, Yuda, are you all right?" "Dad, you know those doves we saw outside the temple?" "Right, I remember." "They were $30, right." "Yes…," replied Meshel. "The doves in here are $560!" "Right, Yuda. I meant to explain that to you." "How can that be!?!" Yuda exploded. Meshel said, "You see these animals that are for sale inside the temple are guaranteed to be accepted by the inspector for sacrifice, while the ones bought outside are almost certain to be rejected."

Yuda frowned and said, "You mean there is an inspector of the animals?" "Yes," replied Meshel, "to make sure they are perfect for the sacrifice." "That sounds a little strange to me," said Yuda. "Well we want to make sure we do things right," said Meshel. "Wait," said Yuda, "does that cost, too?" "Well, now that you mention it, there is a fee, yes." "Dad, this doesn't seem right to me! Somebody ought to do something!"

Lemel indicated just then, that he was about ready to open. He pointed across the temple area to a group that had just come in. "You see those folks?" he asked. "Yes," Meshel said, "who are they?" "That's a new rabbi, Jesus, that has been gaining a reputation here. He's not well liked by the authorities. He's with his disciples." As they watched, the rabbi said something to one of his followers and went back out.

Lemel had opened by now and helped Meshel with the money he needed. Meshel stayed a few moments to chat with Lemel about what had been happening in Jerusalem, when suddenly the rabbi came back. He looked different. Yuda thought he had never seen anyone so angry. His face reminded Yuda of what he remembered of the story of Mount Sinai and God producing thunder and lightning. Then Yuda and Meshel realized that Jesus had made a whip and was shouting at the merchants in the temple.

Time suddenly froze for Yuda. Jesus was cracking the whip and driving all the animals out of temple. He was shouting at the merchants to get out of the temple. He went over to the dove sellers and pointedly told them to take the doves and leave. Then he came over to the money changers and as he strode along, he turned over their tables and scattered all the money across the floor of the temple. Everyone's money got mixed up and went flying all over. He came over to Lemel's table and everyone got out of the way as everything went flying.

Yuda and Meshel saw Jesus' face filled with outrage, his eyes were blazing, and he was saying, "Stop making my Father's house a place of business!"

All the people were running out of the temple, and when Meshel and Yuda had gotten to a quieter place outside, Yuda asked his father, "Dad, what happened!? What about the sacrifice?" "Yuda," Meshel said with emotions of awe and some satisfaction, "I think you got your wish! I think we saw something more important than a sacrifice. I think… someone finally did something!"

11. Listen to Who?

As Tovi was walking into the town of Sychar, she met her friend Dobah. "Tovi! Have you heard the news? She's getting married again!"

"Who is getting married again?"

"Why Dassi, of course. Can you believe it?"

"How many husbands does this make?" asked Tovi. "I think this is five. Might be four, but I think it's five," answered Dobah. "She doesn't seem to care about who she is or what people think about her."

Tovi and Dobah went on to discuss the news of the day in Sychar and in Samaria in general. It was a normal beginning to a day for the two friends.

It was some months later that they had an occasion to discuss Dassi again. "Tovi, I don't know if it's better or worse." "You mean Dassi getting rid of her husband, Dobah?" "Yes, and then what I heard is that she has another man she's living with, but she's decided not to marry this one." "I see what you mean, Dobah. Hard to tell if that's an improvement or not. Wonder what's next?"

What happened next was not exactly what the two were expecting. It was a few months later when Tovi and her husband, Birach, were in town. Birach was discussing a few things with some other men when Tovi nudged her husband. "Look!" she said. The men looked up, and one of them said, "Don't look at her, maybe she'll go away."

But Dassi didn't go away. She kept coming toward them. Short of running off in several different directions, they had

49

no choice but to resign themselves to having to meet the infamous woman of Sychar.

"Birach, Tovi! I need to tell you what happened to me!" Dassi exclaimed. "Dassi, I don't think …" started Birach. But Dassi was running right on. "It's this man I met. I was at the well drawing water, you know, and he talked to me."

"Merciful heavens," thought Birach, "not again." "No!" said Dassi, reading his thoughts. "This is different! He asked for water. I thought this Jewish man asking a Samaritan woman was amazing. But I thought I should at least try to help him. Then he started talking about 'living water' and I asked him where he was going to get this crazy water that you don't get thirsty again and life is eternal."

"Dassi wait, I really think …" started Birach.

"No! Listen! That's when he told me everything about myself! This stranger. He's never been here before, I would have known. (I'll bet you would, thought Birach.) He knew about my husbands. He knew about my current …, well situation. So, I thought, well he must be some kind of prophet. And to get on a more comfortable topic, I brought up about worship, and, you know, how those Jews think people should only worship down in Jerusalem. He picks up on that and says God is spirit and something about worshiping him as spirit. So naturally I said, well that I knew about Messiah coming—I'm not dumb. And that's when he said it!"

There was a pause, as if Dassi was waiting for a response, so Birach asked, "Um, said what, Dassi?"

"Didn't I say? He said he's the one. He's the Messiah. That's how he knew all about me. Birach, you're up on this stuff. I know I'm probably worse than nobody to you. But I know you're clear about the real important stuff. Could this be him? Could this be Messiah? Birach—he told me everything about me. Everything! Come! Talk to him!"

Well, of course, Birach had little choice at that point, and he was curious even if it was Dassi. So, he and Tovi and a couple other men went with Dassi to the town well.

They found a group of men sitting by the well, as if they were waiting for Dassi to return. "This is him!" Dassi said, leading them to Jesus.

"Hello Birach, Tovi," said Jesus. "I see Dassi has convinced you to come with her."

"How do you know about Dassi?" started Birach, when he realized what Jesus had said and went on, "Wait! How do you know about us?"

"Thank you for coming, Birach," said Jesus. "This could take some time. I would like a chance to talk to you. There are some things I'd like to share with you. These are my disciples, by the way. They've been with me for a while, now."

Birach looked at Tovi and the other men, took a deep breath, and said, "Would you please come into town with us so we can hear what you have to say?" "Of course," said Jesus, "good idea."

So, Jesus and the disciples walked with Birach, Tovi, the men with them, and Dassi (just a little ways back) into the town of Sychar. Over the next two days, Jesus spoke to people in the town and listened to them. It didn't take long for the townspeople to realize that they were very blessed with Jesus coming and talking to them.

By the end of the second day, before Jesus and his disciples took their leave from the townspeople, Birach took Dassi aside. He said, "Dassi, when you first came and talked to us, I thought you were crazy. Then I thought I better find out who this was who had come. Listening to you made me think it was possible that Messiah had come. But now... well, now I know. We all know. We have listened to Jesus, and we know that he is Messiah, our Savior."

"I'm so glad," said Dassi, not too sure what else to say.

"Also," said Birach, "I think you have changed. I'm never going to avoid you again. I can see that Jesus has touched your heart and made a difference in your life. You are an important person in our town, now."

"Me!" said Dassi.

"Yes, you. When you met Jesus, you not only believed him. You came and got us. Our lives have been changed because of you. You could have left us out because of the way we always treated you, but you didn't. You included us. Now, we have a life with hope, with joy that goes beyond what we have and what we do. We have been changed as you have been changed. I, and the rest of the town, owe you a lot. I want you to know that."

"Wow!" said Dassi.

Just then Jesus and his disciples passed by, going on their way, and Dassi called after them, "Thanks, Jesus!"

12. He's Not Coming

After the usual weekly meeting when Baruch, Herod's administrative assistant, gave updates to the office team about Herod's somewhat ephemeral priorities, Baruch found himself talking to his colleague, Leibish.

"You look like you're dragging a little, Baruch," Leibish said. "It's been a difficult couple of weeks," Baruch responded. "My son, Shachne, has been very sick. I have to tell you I've been worried a lot."

"Have you taken him to the doctor?" "We've got an appointment this afternoon, so I'm hoping we can get some good results. My wife, you know Minka, says we should go see this preacher Jesus. Says he sometimes heals people, too."

"Baruch! You do know that would be an extraordinarily bad idea—I mean considering where we work, right?" "I know. I know," said Baruch. "So, I am hoping for something definite from the doctor."

It was a few days later that Leibish saw Baruch again. "How's that son of yours, Baruch?" Then he realized the answer was pretty obvious from the way Baruch looked. "Shachne is much worse. We've been back to the doctors. They've given up. I'm at my wits end."

"You need some time off, Baruch? I'll cover for you if you'd like." "Yes, I think that's what it has come to. Minka heard that the preacher, Jesus, is coming to Cana. She thinks he can help if he wants to. I'm not so convinced. But Shachne… well, … I've got to try, at least. You take the meeting this week, tell everyone I have some family issue."

"Baruch! That's really dangerous. You know that." "Yes," Baruch sighed. "I know. But right now I have no other choice. This Jesus is my last resort."

The next morning Baruch and Minka told Shachne what they were planning to do before Baruch left. Shachne seemed to be slipping away. It was with a heavy heart that Baruch took his personal servant Yudel with him and set off to travel the twenty miles from Capernaum to Cana.

Yudel was used to helping Baruch, and on the way he asked him, "How will you find this Jesus, sir?" "I am hoping that he is known well enough that I can ask someone in Cana if they know where he is." "Will he know what an important person you are, sir?" Baruch almost chuckled, "I rather doubt that, Yudel."

It was in the afternoon when Baruch and Yudel came into Cana. Baruch was looking for someone to ask about Jesus, when he realized that there were a lot of people heading to the other edge of town. He and Yudel followed them, and there, in a field, was a man in the middle of a crowd.

The people who were gathered seemed to be country folks or towns people, but no one who appeared to be wealthy or influential. As Baruch approached the edge of the crowd, a few people recognized him because of his office, and made way for him to come through.

As they got close to the center, they could see that Jesus was talking to individuals and putting his hands on them. There seemed to be a line of those waiting for a chance with Jesus. Those who saw him, left with a satisfied smile on their faces.

It took a lot of effort for Baruch to wait in line with Yudel. As they slowly approached Jesus, Yudel asked, "What will he do, since your son is not with us?" Just then a way opened

54

up, and several people got out of the line to make way for Baruch. Baruch thought of all those who had left Jesus blessed and smiling. He took a deep breath, came, and kneeled before Jesus. The crowd became quiet. Some gasped in amazement.

Baruch introduced himself, and explained that his son was critically sick in Capernaum. He said, "I can see sir, that you are a caring man, and have the power to heal people. I beg you, lord, to come and heal my son." He looked at Jesus and found it difficult to decide what Jesus was feeling.

So, Baruch started again, and begged Jesus to come, saying that his son was at the point of death. He implored Jesus to come with him because Jesus was their only hope.

To his great surprise, Jesus did not seem to look very friendly or open to coming to Capernaum. Then Jesus said, "You won't believe unless you see signs and wonders." There was shuffling behind Baruch as if others wanted to take his place. But Baruch looked in Jesus' eyes. They didn't seem to be antagonistic.

Again, Baruch, still kneeling down, bowed before Jesus, and said, "Sir. Come, before my son dies." His voice had strength, but shook from tense emotion.

It was quiet again. Baruch looked up. Jesus had a strange look on his face. He looked directly at Baruch and said, "Your son lives."

Jesus was quiet then. He looked deeply into Baruch's eyes. Then he looked away to the next person in line. Just before Jesus turned to talk to the next person, he looked back at Baruch with a questioning look.

Baruch opened his eyes wide, stood up straight, and smiled. He began to breathe again. He gave up his plan, and accepted Jesus' plan. He found himself believing what Jesus had said. Baruch looked at Jesus again and saw a look of wonder on his face.

Yudel had been close but found it hard to understand what had happened. "Will he come, sir?" Yudel asked. "No, Yudel, he isn't coming." "I'm so sorry, sir," Yudel exclaimed. "Not necessary," said Baruch, "he doesn't have to." "What!" exclaimed Yudel. "Come," said Baruch, "it's late, we're going to spend the night. We'll head back in the morning."

Yudel was confused by Baruch's attitude but followed and saw to his master's needs for the night.

The next morning, they got up early and set off going back to Capernaum. The twenty miles seemed a long way to Yudel, but Baruch seemed to have left all stress behind. As they got close to home, Tilleh, Minka's personal servant, came running toward them. "Master! He doesn't have to come! Your son is better!"

"Listen!" Baruch interrupted. "When did he start to get better?" Tilleh spluttered a few times, "It was … I think … let me think … you mean when …, well, it was about 3 pm yesterday afternoon, sir."

Baruch smiled broadly at Yudel and Tilleh, and asked "Yudel, when did Jesus talk to me?" Yudel, now smiling, too, said, "Yes, master, it was about 3 pm."

"Yes, that's when he said it," Baruch said almost quietly. "You saw this Jesus, sir?" Tilleh asked. "He told you your son would recover? He told you there was hope? Did he say he might not die?" "No," said Baruch, "he said, 'Your son lives.'"

It was sometime later that the family was together all celebrating the wonderful blessing of Shachne's healing.

Baruch's wife asked, "What was he like, this Jesus?" Baruch repeated again, "He said, 'Your son lives'." "And you believed him," said Minka. "Yes. He didn't just talk. He didn't encourage. He didn't extend compassion. He spoke those words and his eyes said that his words made it happen. I believed him."

"So do I," said Minka. "Not just about Shachne. I believe his saying those words touched more than Shachne. You realize we've been changed. We're different, now. Why?"

"Yes, my position is not the most important thing in our lives. And Shachne, not even you are most important now. We believe something… No. We believe Someone who has changed the rest of our lives."

13. A Long Second

Yefet was speaking to those gathered in the synagogue at Nazareth. He introduced Jesus, the local boy who had been traveling around the country. Some reports were that he had done amazing things that some called miracles. Yefet thought it was really respectful that he remembered his roots and came to his hometown this Sabbath.

Yefet handed Jesus the scroll of Isaiah. He thought Jesus should be able to find something he would like to share with them from the great book of Isaiah.

Zev was thinking about the table he had that Jesus had made. Very nice table, he thought. He looked across the room and saw Shaul, one of the teachers Jesus had particularly liked. Shaul was certainly smiling today. He'll probably want to take credit for anything good that Jesus has to say, Zev thought.

People in Nazareth were proud of Jesus. They didn't quite understand what had become of him these last few years. Zev remembered some of the gossip that he had heard saying that Jesus had gotten above himself, going around the country and talking to large groups of people. Well he was here now. Jesus could help everyone feel at ease.

Zev liked the passage Jesus chose. It was one of his favorites. It seemed so positive and hopeful about God finally blessing his people. And considering all that has been going on around our country, thought Zev, sometime soon would be really great!

Wait, he was coming to the end. Zev wondered what Jesus would have to say about this passage. "Fulfilled in your hearing." That sounds really encouraging, thought Zev.

Sounds like Jesus agrees with me that soon would be good. He saw others around the synagogue nodding in approval. Looked like they thought so, too. Joseph's son. Joseph would have liked to live to see his son here.

What was he saying? Something about doing some miracles here? Well, of course, there had been some talk about that. If Jesus could make people well, there were some here, sure enough, who could use his help.

No prophet accepted? Oh, I think, Zev thought, that we accept you, Jesus, as a real fine prophet. Haven't seen you do a lot of prophet stuff, but I think we're open to that, all right. We like young people to grow up and make something of themselves, that's for sure.

Now that didn't sound so good about Elijah and Elisha helping those outside of Israel instead of the chosen people. Wait! thought Zev, I think he really means fulfilled. He wants us to believe that he is the one. The real thing. The promised One. Zev could see that others were thinking the same thing, and the crowd was getting negative and even angry. Apparently, they didn't mind seeing a local boy doing well, but claiming to be the Messiah, well that was a bit too much, really.

As Zev looked around, he saw that people's anger was beginning to boil, some had already started to push Jesus toward the door. Others were getting into place to join in. Zev thought that was to be expected as long as it didn't get out of hand.

But as Zev watched, it was getting out of hand. The angry people in the synagogue were not only pushing Jesus out the door, they were pushing him toward the cliff at the edge of town only a couple blocks from the synagogue.

Yefet came up to Zev and said, "That really was too much. Something had to be done! You agree, don't you Zev?" "Well," said Zev, "it did seem quite extreme, but I hope we can keep some calmness." "Way beyond that," said Yefet. "That Jesus is going to come to a swift end of his prophet work today!"

As Zev started to reply, he saw that Yefet had joined the group pushing Jesus toward the cliff. What was going to happen? How could Jesus say such outrageous things and expect people to take it?

While he watched, he saw Jesus close to the edge of the cliff when suddenly the people stopped. Jesus had turned toward them, ignoring the cliff behind him. He wasn't saying anything, he was just looking at them. Sure enough, some people were getting out of his way. As he looked at people a way opened up for him to walk through the crowd.

Zev realized he was coming toward him and saw Jesus looking at him. Jesus looked like he was walking through the crowd with a power in his step, in his movement, in his eyes that was frightening to see.

Jesus was looking at Zev, and Zev said in his heart, Oh, Jesus, don't look at me that way! What is happening, thought Zev. He's looking right inside me.

Yes, I remember you, Jesus. You loved coming to the synagogue. You loved learning. It was amazing the way you loved your parents and even showed that you liked them, too. Yes, I remember how eager you were to learn from Joseph. And you enjoyed being with Mary and even enjoyed learning to cook from her. You were always amazed that there were children who didn't love their parents and let everybody know it.

Yes, I remember the way you used to sit with Malki. She was, well, she was different. A lot of people made fun of her. She used to sit for hours and just look at flowers. But you went to her and sat with her. For hours. You smiled at her, and she smiled back, and you both just looked at flowers like they were singing some great song that only you could hear.

You were so creative with wood. Joseph was good. Then you seemed to have designs and ways of handling wood that made the tables and chairs and cabinets and everything you made treasures for the people who got them.

You came, yes, I remember to visit me when I was sick. In your twenties you were then. And sat with me. You listened to me. I went on and on about how I felt, and what I wanted to do yet. You're a great listener, that's for sure.

You enjoyed discussing the Word. You made it seem like there was a conversation with God. Some of those people who got so angry—they were there. I remember.

Now you've been around. You're famous. But Messiah? Really, Jesus? Messiah is coming I know, we all know. But not now! A boy from Nazareth? Really? You're good with the word, but The fulfillment? The One from God?

What is happening, thought Zev? What have I been doing? Remembering all that. Jesus is still looking at me, in me. Has it been an hour? No! the crowd hasn't moved! It's only been a second or so.

Who are you, Jesus? I'm afraid if you raise an eyebrow I'll fall on my knees before you.

But no, as he watched, Jesus looked away and went on his way. You're gone, thought Zev. I'm still here. Could I have been wrong? Wrong all this time? Didn't I know you?

14. Second Chance

It wasn't a long trip. The twenty miles had only taken a couple of days. Now Zev got to his brother's place in Capernaum.

Elya was surprised to see Zev. It had been a while since they had visited. "Dear Zev," Elya said at the door, "to what do I owe this brotherly visit?"

"I know," said Zev. "It isn't that far. I should come more often. You came to visit me that time a year ago. It's just… well it seemed like a good time to get away, and I wanted to talk to you. I had this experience…"

They went in and Zev told his brother about his strange experience at the synagogue in Nazareth. He told him that people started off being proud of their native son. But then it had turned to patronizing impatience and finally anger and rejection. Zev explained how he knew Jesus as a child, and how he had been impressed by what Jesus had said. But he felt confused by his feelings and the feelings of his neighbors.

Elya asked Zev, "What does he actually do, then?"

"Well, he goes around teaching a lot. He goes to lots of villages and talks to everyone who will listen."

"Is he grounded in the traditions? Does he agree with our great rabbis?"

"You know, Elya," Zev said, "he doesn't seem that interested in all that. He doesn't refer to the rules and regulations. He doesn't make up new rules to make sure all the old ones are obeyed, the way other rabbis have done."

"But how can he teach then, if he doesn't quote the rabbis?" asked Elya.

"Well, he takes God's word and he just applies it to today. He acts as if God meant part of his word to be for this time, for here and now. He doesn't see the word of God so much as establishing rituals as showing that God is present, and people have an immediate access to his love now."

"What does he do with problems and suffering, then?"

"So this is what I've heard. He heals people."

"Wait! A doctor or a teacher?"

"I've only heard this from others, but yes. The answer is yes. And more. I guess I think now that I've gotten over the experience of him being in the synagogue in Nazareth—I think he's important. To us. But I'm struggling to fit that in with my memories of him as a child living a few blocks away, those years ago. I think he's bringing light from God to people now. I'm just having difficulty seeing how it fits in with what we think of as faithful life as the chosen people of God.

"Well I can see that you need a break Zev," said Elya. Hopefully you'll have a peaceful time here. And by the way, at synagogue last week, Yuda, our synagogue ruler, said we would find this week to be interesting."

"Thanks, Elya, for your understanding. I can use peaceful, normal, traditional, and interesting would be ok, too."

So, the time came to go to the synagogue. They got there early and focused on their traditional prayers. There was the atmosphere of the Capernaum lakeside and the traditions and prayers of the normal synagogue service. Then Yuda came in with the guest speaker and Zev grabbed Elya's arm. "It's him!" he exclaimed.

"You mean ..." started Elya, and Zev replied with a strenuous whisper, "Yes!"

Jesus was introduced by Yuda to the gathered group and thanked them for the opportunity to come. When it was his time to address the group, he spoke with quiet confidence, without hesitation. He took the appointed text and applied it to those who were there. He talked about families, relationships, hopes, politics, friends, problems. As he went on, more and more people seemed to notice that he spoke with confidence without referring to other rabbis, without quoting historical bases for his comments.

Zev heard some whispering, "He seems to speak on his own authority!"

Suddenly Elya gripped Zev, "Oh, no! It's Mendl!" There was tension that spread through the assembly.

The man who had walked in, came up to Jesus, mumbling on the way. Then he shouted, "What business do we have with each other Jesus of Nazareth? Have You come to destroy us? I know who You are—the Holy One of God!"

Zev and Elya looked at each other with a mixture of fear and amazement. Yuda looked like he had a horror-stricken idea that everything was wildly out of control.

Then Jesus took charge.

Jesus spoke sternly and directly, not to Mendl, but to the one inside him, "Be quiet, and come out of him!"

Suddenly Mendl was thrown into convulsions and there was a loud voice shouting. All in the room were stunned to silence until Mendl slowly got up, smiled at Jesus, and said, "Thank you, sir, with all my heart!"

There was a buzz of amazement in the synagogue as Elya turned to Zev and said, "OK, that's impressive!" Others in the room were saying, "Such authority!" Still others, "He teaches with authority and speaks to our needs and the spirits obey him!"

Jesus quieted the room and brought his teaching to a conclusion. Then as Yuda, the synagogue ruler, dismissed the group, Jesus talked to some of the people who came over to him.

Zev went to Mendl and said, "I'm sorry, I knew you weren't well. It's been some years, but I should have come to see you." "No," said Mendl, "thank you. It wouldn't have helped. I was not in much condition to see old friends. But now, thanks be to God, I am really blessed and well. Jesus is really amazing! It's so wonderful to be out of that darkness. We'll stay in touch. Forgive me for leaving quickly, but I need to find what's left of my family."

As Mendl hurried out, others were leaving also. Some were mumbling, "I've got to tell …" as they left.

Jesus stopped by Zev, "I understand you have a lake nearby. Are you going to take me out to the lake and push me in?"

Elya had his mouth open with amazement. Zev said, "No, Rabbi Jesus. I was angry, uncertain, confused. Now you have given me a second chance. I didn't deserve it. Thank you. No one has authority like yours. I'm going to listen to you. I'm going to look for a way to listen to you again. I think what I'm going to do is to find a way to follow you."

Jesus smiled at Zev and Elya, put his hand on Zev's shoulder, and as he was leaving said with a quiet, confident authority, "I'm sure you'll find a way."

15. No One (Except...)

Ezriel was well known. For quite a while now, he was one of the few who was in the synagogue every time the doors were open. Ezriel didn't want to take over and tell people what to do, he just felt blessed being part of the fellowship. He really enjoyed being a blessing to others in the synagogue. He didn't want credit—he just, in a quiet way, took in a lot of satisfaction from helping others.

The ruler of the synagogue had told Ezriel, and his mother as well, that he was headed for leadership and important responsibilities in the synagogue. Ezriel just smiled. He didn't really feel a need for being important. But his mother Chava, she really enjoyed talking about him to others. It always started with, "My son, you know my son, Ezriel, ..."

In the midst of this sense of satisfaction and well-being, there came, what seemed like, a strange small event. Ezriel first noticed that his skin had a pale spot. He was outside quite a bit, and his skin was a healthy dark color, except in this one spot. Ezriel thought over time, it would catch up in color to the rest of his arm.

But it didn't.

Instead, it spread to a wider area. Then there was a sense of numbness that grew more and more noticeable. Ezriel started growing concerned when the numbness included a lot of his arm. Up until then he just lived in denial that there was anything serious happening. When he started getting infections that would not easily heal, he knew that he had a serious problem.

Ezriel's arm started to look deformed, and it became difficult to hide from the people around him. Others in the synagogue kept smiling but started to keep a distance from him when they talked to him. It didn't take long before people avoided him when they saw him coming. If he was going to be at a meeting, people suddenly found reasons not to participate.

Ezriel tried hiding the problem. He used ointments. He asked others for advice. Then finally his rabbi asked to meet with him and a priest, Shabtai, from Jerusalem. The priest asked him to show him his arm. He looked at it carefully without touching it. He was quiet for a long time, and then looked at Ezriel with sorrow and grief showing in his usually loving expression.

"Ezriel," he said slowly, "I'm afraid it's time to face the facts." Ezriel found it difficult to listen to what he knew was coming and had tried so hard to avoid thinking about. "You have leprosy, Ezriel," said the priest. Rabbi Yotham said, "I've not wanted to talk to you about it, but the time has come when you will have to make some changes. You are going to have to go live with a group of people who share your disease. You will find them outside of town on the west side. You will need someone to help you by providing you with food and any other necessities."

Ezriel was close to tears as he broke in, "Are you absolutely sure?! Couldn't we wait a while to see if it gets better? Maybe I just need a different diet or …"

"No, Ezriel," said Rabbi Yotham with a conviction that he clearly used without any enjoyment at all. "We have probably waited too long just because you are such a blessing in our midst. But now the time has come when, for the sake of the rest of the synagogue and for the sake of your family, you must leave."

The words were so harsh and so final that Ezriel winced and fell back into the chair. "How long can I take to prepare?" he asked.

"You have to get to the group before sundown tonight, Ezriel. And may God have mercy on you."

With that Rabbi Yotham and Priest Shabtai stood and made it clear that their conversation was over. Ezriel stumbled out and got to his family sobbing and filled with dread. He explained to his mother Chava the horrible truth. After they sat with tears flowing for a while, Ezriel said he needed to get ready. Chava prepared food for him and promised that she would find a way to supply him with the food he needed.

Ezriel found the group without difficulty. There was no enthusiasm in their welcome, just recognition that he was one of them. The grief and fear that went with their situation flattened all emotion to limited basic communication.

The days that followed dragged on for Ezriel and his mother. She would bring food and try not to look shocked at her son's appearance.

As days turned to months, Chava got help from the other members of the synagogue who contributed what food they could to help. Even with the help, the situation looked hopeless.

Ezriel hated his situation. He hated where he was. He hated his body. He hated himself. He somehow felt guilty. He felt like it was all his fault.

Then one day when his mother came, she said she had news that might help. She had heard of someone who was a preacher who also healed people. Ezriel looked at his arms that were withered and deformed. His whole heart was full of despair and hatred of himself. But his mother told him, "Go, ask the preacher for help. For me. Go!"

"I can go," said Ezriel. "I can go but it won't make any difference. No one can help now. If you insist, I'll go. But he won't touch a person like me. He can't undo what I am." "Go!" Chava said quietly with all the emotion she had left.

So, Ezriel painfully went and found the preacher. All the way people avoided him and scattered out of his way. Then, finally he found Jesus. Jesus' followers saw Ezriel coming, and scattered out of his way, too.

Ezriel looked at Jesus expecting Him to do the same when He saw what condition Ezriel was in. But no, to his amazement, Ezriel saw Jesus coming toward him. Jesus wasn't repulsed. He looked at Ezriel as a person! A spark of hope lit in Ezriel's heart. He thought of his mother and fell before Jesus, saying, "Lord if You are willing You can make me clean."

To Ezriel's utter astonishment, Jesus reached out His hand and touched Ezriel's arm and said, "I am willing. Be cleansed!" Ezriel had trouble taking in what had just happened. He looked at his body and it was back to healthy—not just a little better, not on the mend, but well!

Jesus smiled and told him, "Don't tell anyone, Ezriel. Now what you need to do is go and show yourself to the priest according to the law."

Ezriel thought, "It's not over? It might not be finished?!" But then he looked at Jesus' smile and suddenly realized it wasn't an order, it was a privilege. He smiled back at Jesus and said, "Thank you, Gracious Lord. I'm on my way!" With that he set off to find the priest.

It took a while to find the priest Shabtai. All the way there, Ezriel found a sense of joy growing in him. He hadn't realized how much the depression and hatred of himself had consumed him. Now Jesus' touch had not only healed him from the terrible leprosy that was destroying his body. Jesus had also healed him from the hatred, the loathing, the hopelessness, the terrible fear with which he had been living.

By the time he found where the priest Shabtai was located, Ezriel had a sense of great joy at the news he was bringing to the one who had told him there was no hope. No hope! he thought. Wait until I tell him about Jesus. He's in for a surprise!

Ezriel still had some people he needed to tell about the news. Not many, as Jesus had said. Just his mother, the great people at the synagogue, Rabbi Yotham, well maybe there were a few others... .

16. Not Very Nice

Yakov did not have as his life goal to be a cantankerous, arrogant, mean-spirited old man. When he grew up in Capernaum, he enjoyed the small city that was growing on the shore of the Sea of Galilee and wanted to be a success there.

Capernaum was well situated for growth. Besides being on the shore of the lake, it was on the trade route going through Israel. The land around Capernaum was just right for agriculture. So, fruit and vegetables were plentiful as well as fish being available in abundance.

As he grew up, Yakov was well liked and got to know most of the people of the area. There had been a fruit stand in the main part of town for as long as anyone could remember, but Yakov had a plan for making it a major part of the town's business community.

He went to work there and through the years he took more and more responsibility until he was the one running the store. He expanded the building. He welcomed more and more of the surrounding growers to sell their wares in his emporium. He convinced the fishermen that they could get the best price for their catch through his contacts with people.

Yakov started to work with those traveling along the trade route to supply their needs and to sell the products they were bringing from distant lands. His business continued to grow well.

Because of the trade route, there was also a Roman military outpost in the city. So, Yakov contracted with the centurion's procurement officer to supply their needs as well. Yakov was a major retailer in the area, and he was enjoying himself enormously.

That was the beginning of the problem. He enjoyed the money he was making. He enjoyed it a lot.

Yakov started to look for new ways to make more money. Instead of concentrating on the interests of his suppliers and his customers, he started to concentrate on what he could do with the money that was coming in. He built a new, spacious, and luxurious home for himself and his wife. He started to think he needed the various luxury items that appeared on the trade route. And with his change of focus, there came some other changes.

The first change was that he raised his prices by increasing his markup, without paying his suppliers more. He did it slowly, and he found it to be very satisfying. But soon it wasn't enough, and he started reducing what he paid his suppliers so that his income would increase even more. He raised the prices he was charging the military as well.

He kept justifying his actions by saying to his wife that if people wanted what he offered they would pay for it. If people wanted to be included in his network of sales, they would sell through him. His attitudes were slipping from confident to arrogant, but his wife couldn't convince him of the change.

The customers were complaining. The suppliers were dissatisfied. But Yakov didn't pay much attention; he was too busy enjoying spending his profit.

Then the general accountant from Rome came on his annual trip and saw the prices the military was paying for its supplies compared to the prices in other locales. He came to Yakov's office one day and he was not smiling. He explained to Yakov that things were going to change, or his contract would come to an end. Yakov's expostulating and arrogance had no effect on the Roman official, and in the end, Yakov had to give in.

Yakov had become grumpier through the months before, even though he was financially well off. Now he became frustrated and started to have problems with stress and backaches. He had stiffness that wouldn't go away.

Then customers noticed that the military wasn't paying as much for the things they bought and they complained about Yakov's prices also. He struggled to maintain his arrogant attitude but had to give in to them as well. His stress levels were going up, and Yakov lived with a lot more anger and frustration. He had trouble sleeping. He didn't feel well most days. His wife had to help him more than he wanted her to.

When his suppliers demanded an increase in payment as well, Yakov's physical ailments became severe, and he wasn't able to get around very well. He growled at everyone around him. The few friends he had socially and from business started to become distant in their relationship with him. Yakov became more and more isolated and less able to get up and do anything for himself.

Finally, Yakov became completely unable to do anything for himself. He had become paralyzed from all the anger and stress, from all the selfishness and frustration dealing with people. He had a few friends who had continued to care for him through the years, but now he only growled at them as well.

Yakov's wife ran the business now, and what made Yakov really stressed is that she lowered prices, cared about suppliers, and was making much more of a success of the business even if she didn't make a huge profit in the process.

The remaining friends of Yakov were four: Only Tev, one of the fishermen, Hirsch and Didya from the business community, and Berek from a nearby farm, remained. One day Berek called a meeting of the friends to discuss Yakov's situation.

They all agreed Yakov was headed for an early grave. They had all stopped visiting Yakov—they couldn't stand his acting as if he were still in charge of the world and snarling with frustration. But they also agreed that they remembered the Yakov they had known and enjoyed and cared about. They couldn't think of how to change the situation.

Then a few weeks later, Berek heard about a traveling preacher who was going around Israel proclaiming good news and showing real care for all who came to hear him. Berek even heard that there were some people who were healed of their diseases. That was enough for him. This Jesus was coming to Capernaum, and Berek sent messages to the other friends that now was the time to do something.

The four of them got together on a day that Jesus was meeting with people in a home in Capernaum. They decided it was now or never. They went to Yakov, and without any explanation, they bundled him up (grumbling and snarling), put him on a stretcher they had made, and carried him to the house where Jesus was talking.

To their great disappointment, the crowds were so large, they couldn't get anywhere near Jesus. But Berek wasn't about to stop now. He told the others, "There. Up the stairs to the roof!" So up they went (Yakov yelling at them as much as his weakened body would allow). When they got there, they set Yakov down, and started to take the covering off that sealed the roof. They pulled stuffing from between the beams that made the ceiling. Then they, none too carefully Yakov complained, lowered him through the roof down to where Jesus was talking.

The crowd gathered around Jesus was amazed at the brashness of this interruption. Yakov had suddenly appeared next to Jesus, grumpy and snarling.

Jesus looked at the friends holding the ropes that had lowered Yakov into the room, and he saw their hopeful, expectant smiles. He looked at Yakov, and with a gaze filled with compassion he said to Yakov (with a little more directness than He usually used), "Your sins are forgiven."

There was a brief moment of silence, even from Yakov who showed a mixture of consternation and surprise. Then there was an explosion of words from the pharisees that were present about who had the right to forgive sins. They went on for a while. Yakov meanwhile looked like he was finally touched by what had happened. He was looking at his friends and at Jesus. He was having flashes of his past attitudes and actions in his mind. His heart seemed to be showing signs of thawing.

Finally, he quietly let go. He looked at Jesus as Jesus turned to him and said, "So that you may know that the Son of Man has the authority to forgive sins, I say to you, get up, and pick up your stretcher and go home."

Immediately Yakov became well and strong, completely healed—and he knew it. His friends were silent, holding their breaths. Then Yakov smiled, got off the stretcher, and picked it up. He took a deep breath and still smiling, looked at Jesus, said, "Thank you, Lord. I … I needed that."

There was cheering on the roof, and it spread through the crowd. Jesus was smiling while people in the crowd were saying, "Amazing! Grumpy old Yakov! Smiling! He said, 'Thank you'!! Can you believe it?! Praise the Lord! What a miracle! There is hope after all!"

17. The Doctor's Patients

They grew up together—Matthew and Avram. In school, some students were going through the motions to learn enough to read the Torah for their bar mitzvah, but Matthew and Avram truly enjoyed learning. It seemed to them that the way to have doors of opportunity open for them was to keep learning as much as they could.

Avram, of course, really wanted anything but agriculture as his life work. He wouldn't mind managing a distribution center. Any closer to the actual growing process, though, he didn't want to be.

For Matthew it was different. It probably started with the time he had been given responsibility for the houseplants. "Make sure you water them", he had been told. So he did. Every day. When his older brothers and sisters noticed that the plants had all died, they were convinced that they must keep Matthew away from the family's crops, since obviously Matthew did not have a green thumb. Probably, they thought, it was gray or puce.

Another difference was Matthew's avocation. Once he learned to read, he took God's word as the delight of his life. Any spare moment he was at the synagogue reading. His instructors were proud of him. They had never seen anyone soak up the holy words the way Matthew did.

His favorites were the prophets. He loved to read about the proclamation of God's love for His people. He took in every promise that the prophets spoke. He enjoyed hearing about what God had in mind for the blessing of His people. Matthew used to imagine what it was going to be like when all those promises were fulfilled. What a time to live that would be!

Avram would listen to Matthew's ramblings about how it was going to be. He wasn't opposed to joy and glory in the future, he just thought there wasn't much point to dwell on it now, since everyone knew it was going to be a long time before all that happened. After all it had already been hundreds of years since the prophecies had been spoken.

The subject of employment for Matthew and Avram seemed to cause more difficulty than they had expected. One of the factors was the economy.

The Romans had moved in some years ago. As time went on, it became apparent that they didn't care about the country they were occupying. They only cared about Rome and the economy of the empire. That was the first challenging fact of life.

The second thing was more difficult to specify. There didn't seem to be any positions that Matthew and Avram wanted that would accept them. And the ones that would accept them they didn't want. It was almost as if a door had been closed to them. They tried to be useful in a variety of ways, but without much success. They started talking about what their options were.

It was Avram, one day, who smiling said, "Well, you know, we could work for Rome! We could be tax collectors!" They both laughed for quite a while at that. As they both laughed, they thought that would be beyond the limit of what they would ever consider. But as time went on, and their need for employment grew more pressing, they finally began to discuss the choice more seriously.

As things were, they and their families were not among the strictly "law abiding" population. There were a multitude of small rules about foods and distances they could travel and what they could carry that their families had never quite taken much notice of. As a result, many people who cared a great deal about what the scribes and pharisees thought of them wanted nothing to do with either family, Matthew's or Avram's. They were openly rejected by those who considered themselves "holy". Because they were not alone, it didn't seem to be such a horrible step to consider working for Rome. How much worse could it be, after all?

So, after a lot of thought, Matthew and Avram decided to talk to the recruiter in their town. If they went together, they thought, if it turned out to be a terrible idea, they could have strength to leave and forget about it.

The recruiter turned out to be a very friendly man. He asked them about their situation, and he was very good at listening to them. He expressed compassion for their difficulties. Then he graciously asked them if he could explain their opportunities in Roman service. He was never pushy. He just waxed enthusiastic about their great opportunity ahead. He explained that they could make a very, good living. They could have financial security. They would have a guaranteed future.

Avram asked about what they would need in preparation, and the recruiter assured them that would be a simple process that would not cost them anything at all. Matthew and Avram asked for a few minutes to discuss the offer and stepped outside the office.

Avram asked Matthew what he thought. Matthew said, "I'm surprised to be saying this, but I think this is a good idea. I think this is what we need. It sounds possible." "Yes," said Avram, "I agree. Let's do this." So, they went back in and signed up for the school that would lead them to financial security.

The school turned out to be a lot harder than what it sounded like in the recruiter's office, but they both worked hard and learned what they needed. There were sections on Roman law, Roman occupation policies, principles of taxation, current varieties of taxation, and how to stay abreast of any changes in policies or taxes in the future. The instructor, while genuinely demanding, showed all the students (ten besides Matthew and Avram) a picture of delightful financial success.

The day came when Matthew and Avram graduated and were assigned, fortunately together, to a supervisor for their apprenticeship. The supervisor's name was Marcus, and he welcomed the two in a friendly manner. He told them he would see them the next day and explain their responsibilities.

The next day, the two apprentices noticed a different atmosphere in their training. Marcus laid out their responsibilities. He congratulated them for finishing the schooling (five had dropped out), and he explained that now they would be getting a more realistic picture. They were there, Marcus told them, "To make money!" He told them, "Everything you do is to make money. You are not social workers, counselors, or caring family for the people you meet. You are the law!"

"You will always know what Roman law is requiring from people," Marcus went on, "and your job is to make sure you get that collected from people and as much as you can in addition, so that you make a great income."

Every day as Matthew and Avram came to work, Marcus would send them out to their assignments with the words, "Remember! You are in this business to make a lot of money! For me! And for you! Now go and hold onto that thought!"

So out they went, collecting taxes. And extra. Enough for Marcus' greed, and enough for themselves.

The day came when they were finally finished their apprenticeship with Marcus. They always got the idea that Marcus thought they could have made more money than they did, but he signed off on their credentials, and off they went to work on their own.

Now they didn't have to be quite so greedy, but they did enjoy the idea that they had financial security and a future of success ahead.

It wasn't quite as easy as they had thought in their relations with other people. There were a lot of people who considered them turncoats and traitors. Some stores would not sell to them. A great many people walked on the other side of streets to avoid them. Of course, now, they were also rejected from the temple and not welcome in synagogues. Matthew found that a particularly painful experience. He and the others hadn't consciously rejected God, and now, they just didn't have a chance for much spiritual nourishment.

On the other hand, they found themselves in a new group. They met other tax collectors and their families. They also found themselves in a society of others who were not very concerned about what the Pharisees and scribes thought of them. They were in a group of people who cared about each other and found ways to socialize with each other.

As the years went by, Matthew and Avram settled into a comfortable routine. They didn't have the same greedy attitude that Marcus had, but they still had a lot of financial success. Through the years, though, the motivation for making a lot of money faded significantly for both of them. It didn't look like there were going to be any changes in the foreseeable future for them.

Then one day as they were socializing with others in their group, someone mentioned that they had heard of a new preacher who was traveling around, who didn't seem to care how much people had followed the rules so far in their lives. Feishel and Golda were a couple who had a farm. They were fairly self-sufficient. Matthew had met them a few times. They said they were going to hear this preacher, and Matthew said he would go with them.

The three of them made a day of it, going to the large field where this Jesus was talking. There were some people coming and going, but Matthew, Feishel, and Golda found Jesus interesting to listen to. Afterward, they talked about what they had experienced. Feishel said that if he had learned that attitude toward God as a youngster, he would have been a lot closer to God now. Matthew said that Jesus seemed to be a lot closer to his understanding of the Scriptures' picture of God and His love than any Pharisees or scribes that he had ever heard.

Avram went with them the next time they went to listen and they all agreed that there seemed to be real hope for a spiritual life that didn't depend on keeping hundreds of rules in order to love God and be loved by God. The preacher went on to other places, but the four kept talking about a new hope that they felt because of hearing him.

One day Matthew was at work, and he had done well. He hadn't had to overcharge the poor people who were paying taxes, and the rich people seemed to think Matthew's request of money from them was reasonable even though he was going to make quite a bit for himself.

He was just finished keeping his records up to date, when he looked up and standing there before him was a group of men. As they moved closer, he recognized one as the preacher, Jesus. Matthew started to feel a little uncertain what he could ask for from this group, when Jesus said to him, "Follow me."

In what seemed like an instant, Matthew saw the path he had been on, from delight in God's word, to problems, frustrations, despairing of work, stepping over the line to working for Rome, finding a new group of caring people, having the opportunity to listen to Jesus, and beginning to see hope of a different relationship with God leading to this man standing in front of him, smiling and expectant. To his amazement Matthew realized that Jesus really expected him to follow Him and, that, astounding as it was, he wanted to.

It seemcd like the world was standing stlll, the group with Jesus had gotten quiet, and they were looking at him, too. Matthew blinked a couple times, took a deep breath, and got up. He found as he stood that strength and joy were filling his frame. He smiled at Jesus, and … leaving everything behind, followed Him, not having a clue where they were going.

Somehow during the hours that followed Matthew asked Jesus if He would consider coming to his house for dinner, and Jesus said, "Of course. Great idea! How about Monday of next week?"

Matthew sent word to Avram about what had happened and asked him to please set up a dinner for Jesus and those with Him.

It was a whirlwind couple of days being with Jesus. Matthew had talked to the others following Jesus about how they had come to Jesus. Several described an experience like Matthew's—they had met Jesus, and then there came a time when Jesus invited them to follow Him. For each one, it had been a surprise to be invited. Now, however, it seemed perfectly natural to be going about the country with Jesus. They told Matthew that there were a lot more people whose lives had been changed with great blessings who stayed where they were and just spread the joy they now had in their lives with those around them.

When Monday came, Jesus arrived with Matthew and the rest of those following Him. Matthew wasn't quite sure how many people Avram would invite but he thought there might be some of their friends who might want to come. When he saw his home filled with people and Avram standing by the front door smiling, he started laughing. "I see that you have managed to find a few folks to invite!"

Avram was laughing, too. "I asked some of our friends, but the word spread, and well … here we are!" Matthew introduced Jesus and his new friends to Avram and then just waved his hand and said, "and here are some of our friends and … others!"

During the dinner, Feishel and Golda came up to say hello to Jesus. They were surprised and pleased that Jesus remembered them. That was when the uninvited guests showed up. Golda whispered (none too softly), "Here come the Rule Police!" Feishel frowned and responded, "Shh." By this time the dinner guests were getting quiet, watching to see what was going to happen. Some were wondering if the dinner was going to have to come to a quick end.

The Pharisees went up to some of Jesus' followers and asked, "Why is your Teacher eating with the tax collectors and sinners?" While the followers were trying to explain the dinner, Jesus spoke up and said, "It is not those who are healthy who need a physician, but those who are sick."

Now it was quiet and everyone heard Jesus' words. Matthew and Avram wondered if some people would be offended and leave, but Feishel leaned over and said, "Don't worry, Matthew. Please understand that we know who we are." And apparently that was true because no one got up to leave.

Then they heard Jesus going on, "I did not come to call the righteous, but sinners." At this, the Pharisees affected a look of horror, that most of the people at the dinner thought was really overdone.

For years afterward, that was the night that stood out in the minds of many people as the beginning of hope. Instead of feeling like God had abandoned them because they didn't follow all the rules, they had experienced God coming to them personally and caring about them.

Matthew went off with Jesus and His other followers with a sense of great joy and satisfaction, and for Avram, Feishel, Golda and the others who had been at the dinner, life had also changed forever. They knew they were sinners. But now they knew they had a Doctor who had brought Life to them and … brought them to Life.

18. Any Hope Left?

"Stay away from that crowd!"

That had been what Esdras' mother had said. From an early age, Esdras had been attracted to the group of young people that managed to get in trouble.

He had an older brother, Menke, who was the good son. Menke didn't seem to have trouble doing what his parents wanted. He seemed to like what they had in mind for him. It was just hard for Esdras to understand.

Esdras' father would take him aside and talk to him. He wasn't mean or abusive in his language to Esdras. He worked to explain how there were different paths that people chose in life. Esdras' father would pick out some of the crowd that Esdras enjoyed and show Esdras the consequences that were already happening because of the lifestyle his friends had chosen.

From Esdras' point of view, the consequences were entirely unjust and narrow minded. He would try to explain to his father how life was so much more exciting and satisfying when he was with his crowd of friends. That's when his father would always close his remarks for the day with the heartfelt statement that he so wished Esdras could value from his experience and not have to learn the hard way.

Esdras knew his father and mother cared about him. He just didn't like the, from his point of view, excruciatingly boring life that they (and Menke) had chosen to live.

Esdras grew up and worked hard at the jobs he had, but he could not find any satisfaction except in the crowd of people his parents disliked so intensely. He felt young at heart. He felt a need to be alive and live with all the intensity he had. He felt… really he felt immortal. This was life, he thought, living in excitement with those who focused on satisfying themselves with whatever they wanted.

Esdras got to be very good at selfish living. Life was for satisfying himself! That was his attitude. Nothing bad is going to happen, I'm enjoying myself, he thought.

Esdras' parents prayed for him. However, they could see that he was on a self-destructive path, and what they felt and saw and said and did made no difference to Esdras and his passion for selfish living.

From the point of view of Esdras' parents, he was always selfish. He drank too much. He spent a lot of time with that group that liked to drink too much. He had some friends, but honestly, they could see, he used them. He was not kind to them. He was not a friend to them. He used women. He was selfish, arrogant, and thought only of himself.

Then, of course, there came a time when the money started to run out. His selfishness and pleasure-seeking was costing much more than he was making. And his lifestyle got in the way of his improving his employment prospects.

When the crash came, it was actually a surprise to Esdras. He just could not see where his path was leading. He had continued to spend more than he could pay on his excesses. And finally the collectors who came to him about his bills, decided to make an example of him. They beat him up and crippled him for life.

Esdras might have died soon afterward, but although his parents had died, his brother Menke amazingly still cared about him. Menke found him and did what he could to keep him alive. There wasn't anything Menke could do to fix the damage that Esdras had suffered. But he gave Esdras a place to exist while Esdras turned more and more to hopelessness and despair.

Menke knew about the pool where others with little hope gathered. There was a story that an angel came and stirred the waters at times and whoever got in the water first would be healed of whatever ailed him. Menke had a life to live and work to do, but he figured at least he could take Esdras to this place that had a little hope.

That's how it started. Every morning Menke would take Esdras to the pool of Bethesda and leave him there for the day. Esdras was resigned that it was as good a place as any to wait for life to come to an end.

There were people who jumped in the pool and were blessed, occasionally, but Esdras didn't hold out much hope for that to happen to him. Days went on. Years went on. And decades went on. This was Esdras' existence.

Then a change came in Menke's attitude. He told Esdras that he had heard of a preacher that healed people. He said he would like to take Esdras to him. But as Esdras had been on a downward path in selfishness, he was now on a path of just holding onto existence. Esdras couldn't see any way to change that, and he told Menke that he really was too old, too tired and too guilty to be interested.

More days and weeks passed, when one day Jesus showed up at the Bethesda pool. To Esdras, it seemed like a strange day—a group of men who looked rather healthy, coming to the pool. Coming to pity us? That's what Esdras wondered.

Strangely, Jesus looked around the pool and came over to Esdras. It was as if he knew Esdras and was looking for him. Esdras had spent a lot of years in depression and discouragement and guilt, so when he looked up at Jesus, his suspicions of Jesus' intent were mostly negative.

Then Jesus asked him the question. "Do you wish to get well?" Esdras was still imagining Jesus as someone looking for a poster person for some charity deal. So, he gave him a fairly evasive answer about no one around to put him in the pool.

Esdras' thinking went down a dark alley into…what would I hope for? I have an endless downhill existence that is my fault. No one can undo what I have done. No one can change this darkness where I live. "Get well"? Are you serious?! What in the world would 'well' look like for me now?!

Esdras saw that Jesus was still looking at him. He thought Jesus would have gone away by now. Then he saw that Jesus was even smiling at him. What in the world was there to smile at anyway?

It seemed as if Jesus' words were echoing in his ears and heart. There appeared to be a kindness in his voice. The question that Jesus had asked seemed to be getting louder in Esdras' memory. Some of the darkness of his life was cracking. Jesus' voice had a strength in it that reached out to him in just remembering Jesus' question.

Now Jesus talked to him again, "Get up, pick up your pallet, and walk." Power was coming from somewhere that made Jesus' words more than an invitation. They were a powerful directive, a command, a tearing open of darkness and hopelessness.

Esdras experienced in his body a change. What had not worked for decades was beginning to work again. Esdras recognized the strength in Jesus' words to him. Beyond his understanding, he reached out and relied on that word of

Jesus'. Without consciously thinking about faith, he took action with the strength of Jesus' words to him and got up. And then what? He was supposed to pick up his bed—there was no turning back now, he would not be coming here again. Esdras found that he could indeed walk.

The way ahead didn't seem very clear. The future was scary and wide open. Yet there was faith growing in Jesus' words. He looked at Jesus and Jesus' face seemed to be sending him on, out of the darkness in which he had been living at the pool of Bethesda. So out he walked into the city, not as a burden to be carried, but as a participant.

He wasn't sure where he was going, but it was a new and scary experience to just walk. He had to start by finding his brother and tell him what had happened. All of a sudden, a group of Pharisees stopped him. "You know what you're doing is illegal! It's the Sabbath! It is not right to be carrying your bed!"

Esdras had a fuzzy recognition that there was a reality he had entered without much thinking. He said, "The man who healed me told me to." The Pharisees wanted to know who this (encourager to lawbreaking) person was. But truly Esdras did not know.

As he was puzzling over what he had said to the Pharisees, (was it his selfishness again, blaming his healer?), Jesus walked up to him as if he had been looking for him again.

Esdras wondered if he would ask how it felt to be walking. Maybe he would give Esdras an agenda of how to restart reality. Maybe he would just give a word of encouragement.

What Jesus said was, "Behold, you have become well; do not sin anymore, so that nothing worse happens to you."

Then he heard Jesus' followers mention his name. And still in something of a fog, (what had Jesus said? Don't sin anymore. Well, I admit that applies to me. Was I really thinking of going back to that?! Seems a little harsh to hear those words though.) Esdras went back to the Pharisees and told them it was Jesus who had healed him.

Esdras stopped to wonder why he had done that. Why had he been so quick to tell them it was Jesus? Was it because he didn't like being told not to go back into sin? Really though, Esdras thought, I have had enough of that, haven't I? Or was it because he was walking into a new world, and it seemed a lot harder than just pitying himself and living in depression? Or was it because he was very glad to know who Jesus was and glad to have an opportunity to let them know: It was Jesus!

Ok, he admitted to himself, he wasn't sure he knew which of those was the reason. But he remembered the caring smile Jesus had even when he gave Esdras that honest, clear direction in the newness of this life he was entering. He had a growing suspicion that Jesus was going to find a way to lead him through this foggy time in his mind and heart to a time of light and, yes, unselfishness—to an entirely different and vibrantly new life. Jesus had given him a second chance at life. What was this new life going to be like? All Esdras knew was that, with Jesus' help, it was going to be much better than the first try.

19. Do What on the Sabbath?

My father shared the rules of the Sabbath. But it was my mother who taught me how to keep the Sabbath.

At the time I thought everyone had the same experience. Not exactly! This is the story of the "not exactly".

My father would call me, "Eber, I want to talk to you." That meant it was time to learn something. Sometimes it hurt to learn because it meant I had to make some changes in my life. But sometimes I felt like I was entering a brighter world than before, growing in understanding.

Several times, the learning was about what to do on the Sabbath. There was the synagogue where we went to be close to the Lord. On the sabbath we would listen to God's word read, and then someone would explain to us what that meant. My father explained to me that it wasn't just at the synagogue that we thought about God's word. When we got home, my mother and sister and I would sit and listen as my father explained what his experiences were and what the reading of the day meant to him in his experience and what he thought it would mean to us all.

So, you can see, we were faithful in keeping the Sabbath. Of course, my mother had some practical ideas about the Sabbath that expanded somewhat on what my father said.

She knew quite a few people who, according to her view, "needed a little encouragement". That's what she used to say. It seemed perfectly plain that the Sabbath was the day to take care of them. She would tell me that the Sabbath is for doing things that reflect the purpose of the Sabbath:

having time with God and being grateful for His grace and mercy. So, when I was old enough, she would tell my father that we would be gone for a little while (to which my father would smile and not ask where we were going). She would get some food that she had prepared and out we would go.

She knew the way to those she would visit very well. She had a plan worked out. Each person had their Sabbath day in the month. We would start walking and she would count our steps. When we got near 2000 (just in case we miscounted) we would start walking backwards for the next part, again until we got close to 2000. We kept that up until we reached the people my mother wanted to help. On the return trip we used the same plan.

After I did this with my mother several times, she asked me if I thought it was right to help people on the Sabbath the way we were doing it. I told her, "Yes, I think it is." She smiled and said, "So do I."

Not everybody I knew had the same experience. My friend Liman had a different experience with the Sabbath. His father taught him the distance permitted to travel on a Sabbath day. If there were things needed on the Sabbath, they had to be prepared the day before. If something fell off a table or someone dropped something, it had to stay where it was until the next day. If a person went outside to move something, it could only be moved 6 feet at most. There were a lot more restrictions. I can't remember them all. Liman had trouble remembering them also, and he sometimes got in trouble for that.

My own experience (which I didn't share with anyone until recently) was that I enjoyed the Scriptures so much, I would create a dance to celebrate that part of God's word. I don't remember all of them, but I still enjoy some of them. I think my mother would have enjoyed them, I'm not sure about my father, and Liman's family—I doubt very much that they would accept that kind of expression of joy.

Part of the Sabbath experience was time for prayer. What I really liked about prayer is that we as a community or a family or even as an individual—we could talk to the Lord, enjoy His company, thank Him for His blessings, and turn over to Him all the things that concerned us. We could have the confidence that He was quite capable of dealing with all our concerns.

I admit that when I prayed about various concerns I would (in a nice friendly way) explain to God what I thought needed to be done. At the same time, I knew that I could leave all those things in God's hands even if He didn't quite follow my plans in the answer He gave.

During the years I saw the Lord give His mercy and answer prayers in a variety of ways. Once my father was very ill, and the Lord graciously brought him back to complete good health. My grandmother had a lot of problems connected to getting old and God saw to it that she was taken care of.

One of our neighbors had a cousin that was healed by a preacher that was traveling around the country. The most difficult time I had was when my friend Liman had something happen to his hand. It got stiff and twisted. He just couldn't use it at all. There were some people who were kind to him and his family; I kept praying for him. It was so difficult for him.

My mother told me of a time that showed God also wanted us to do what we could to help ourselves. She had a good friend, Keila whom she saw often. Keila's husband was Bendet, a Pharisee, who was greatly concerned with knowing and keeping the law at all times and especially on the Sabbath. So, there was this one time on a Sabbath, one of Bendet's sheep fell into a hole at the edge of a field. It

94

wasn't hurt badly, it just couldn't get out. Oh, the noise it made! So Bendet went out and pulled the sheep out of the hole, which I'm sure the sheep appreciated. And Bendet and Keila appreciated the quiet.

I was reminded of that on a Sabbath that brought lasting joy to me. I was in the synagogue; I was focused on prayer. Liman was also in the synagogue preparing for our worship time. Bendet came in with some other Pharisees. They looked very angry considering where we were. Then in came a Rabbi with his disciples. Bendet went over to him to talk to him and got louder and louder.

It seemed they were talking about whether it was all right to do good and heal on the Sabbath. I heard them say this Rabbi's name was Jesus. Bendet was loudly saying that healing on the Sabbath broke the Sabbath rules. Then I heard Jesus say, "What man is there among you who has a sheep, and if it falls into a pit on the Sabbath will he not take hold of it and lift it out? Is it lawful to do good and even heal on the Sabbath?"

As I watched, Bendet's expression turned from anger to outrage.

Suddenly Jesus looked over, saw Liman, and called to him to come over to them. When Liman did, Jesus said, "Stretch out your hand!" Of course Liman couldn't do that. While I was wondering if Jesus knew that, I saw Liman look at Jesus and at his hand. Then he just stretched it out! Liman's expression went from confusion to wonder to confidence.

At this point, I was really astonished. I had prayed a lot for Liman, and I had begun to adjust my directions to the Lord to just help Liman deal with the problem. And here, before my eyes, the Lord answered my prayers (and I'm sure Liman's too). I came over to Liman and celebrated with him for such a great blessing.

But then, I saw Bendet. I have never seen rage like the expression on his face. He looked like he might explode on the spot. He and the other Pharisees stormed out of the synagogue.

I looked at Liman who looked like he was still in a time of joyful surprise. Then I looked at Jesus. He looked really exasperated. But then I saw him take a deep breath and sigh. His expression softened. He looked at me and asked, "Would you like to answer the question?" "You mean is it lawful? Yes. Yes, Sir. I think it's lawful to do good and heal on the Sabbath." Jesus smiled.

After a moment he started walking away, and I heard him say, "So do I."

20. Everything?

Octavia was proud of her husband, Maximus. He was a centurion and had served Rome for seventeen years.

Their son Marcus was growing up well. Admittedly, Octavia and Maximus had expected Marcus to be more interested in sports. Marcus did enjoy being outside. He liked hiking the hills around Rome with his parents. But he really liked learning.

It was a shock when Maximus was killed while on duty in the northern territories. Octavia felt like a large part of her had died with him. It was frustrating for Marcus to be with other teenagers who had fathers at home. Another frustration Marcus felt was a need to take care of his mother.

Quintus, a centurion who had known Maximus well, checked up on Octavia and Marcus and made sure they had what they needed. Marcus grew to respect Quintus and to admire him. So, when Marcus got to the age when he qualified, he followed his father and Quintus into the service.

Octavia felt lost with her son gone, too. But Marcus assured his mother that he would always take care of her. As the years went by, and Marcus advanced in responsibility in the service, he kept his promise, making sure that there was always someone to take care of her. That was when Marcus found Titus, a skilled and caring servant, whom he hired to make sure his mother was well cared for.

Through his military training, Marcus learned new skills. He grew in physical strength and in listening to his superior officers. He learned dedication to his work, and the beginning of tactical thinking.

As Marcus had more varied assignments, he grew to understand the concept of limited authority. Those he worked with and those who supervised them had authority, but only in certain areas. He learned his limits and the limits of others. He heard the maxim frequently, "Nobody is in charge of everything!" Of course, sometimes he wished he could be in charge of more things, but there was comfort in the limit also. If there happened to be a problem outside his control, he knew it wasn't his problem.

Marcus became adept at being responsible in the authority he had, and his superior officer recommended him for advancement. He was particularly good at letting others be in charge of their areas of responsibility, even if he sometimes thought that he could have done better.

Marcus got to know the other soldiers and what their backgrounds were. He learned to listen to others when the opportunity arose. He was especially interested in what motivations other soldiers had for being in the service. So, in the course of time, with his abilities and training, Marcus became a centurion.

In the years of his service, Marcus had known many centurions, and he had formed some opinions about the style of leadership that he preferred. He was not impressed with those who were loud, offensive, and bullying in their leadership. He rather preferred reaching goals and being productive in leadership by caring about his soldiers.

Marcus taught his company of about one hundred soldiers to focus on their responsibilities. He reminded them of the old saying he had learned that "No one is in charge of everything." He listened to each soldier in his unit and showed them respect.

When it came to drilling, Marcus showed his soldiers that he expected a lot from them. They came to a point of having pride that they were in his company because of the respect that they received from him. They learned from Marcus the priorities: Rome, the military, and their unit. One of the areas that Marcus taught that was unique to him was how to serve the people around them with respect.

When their unit was not fighting in a battle, they often were serving to preserve safety and law and order. Marcus considered the people they were serving to be important and taught his men the same attitude. As a result, Marcus and his unit received several awards. And one day, Marcus was called in by his supervising officer for a special request.

Marcus listened to a description of a need for a unit to serve, according to his supervisor, in the "difficult and challenging country, Israel." Marcus was told, that of all the units available at the moment, his was the most qualified to face the challenge. Marcus thought about how well trained his soldiers were, and with very little hesitation agreed to head for Israel.

As Marcus went to talk to his soldiers, he considered the motivations and training that they had. In his speech to them, he emphasized how they would satisfy their motivations of service and personal advancement. He also focused on the people they would serve and the need to get to know them and respect them. With that preparation they headed off to one of the least popular Roman assignments.

When they settled in, Marcus personally led his unit to respect those they were serving by getting acquainted with the Jewish people in Capernaum. At first, they showed that they thought Marcus was clearly their enemy. But they began to soften when he asked them about what they considered the important needs of their community. They discussed the needs for safety and the need for Romans not to intrude into their customs. Then they mentioned the need to rebuild their synagogue. To their utter amazement,

Marcus agreed to contribute a very large amount of money for the project. From that time on, Marcus was truly viewed as a friend of the community.

Of course, Marcus had received a very substantial bonus for coming on this assignment (as had his soldiers). Still, Marcus showed real compassion and understanding by giving so much to the Jewish community.

When Marcus had agreed to the new assignment, his mother had complained a lot until Marcus explained that she was welcome to come along with Titus caring for her in the new land. It took a while for Octavia to feel the adventure and enthusiasm of being with her son, but she did manage, finally, to agree that it sounded like a great plan.

So, it was with Octavia and Titus that Marcus came to his new home. It didn't take long for Octavia to make herself at home with a new climate, new foods, and new friends (especially after Marcus made the gracious donation to the Jewish community.)

Trouble, when it came, was not from the new land and its customs, but from an attack of sickness that Titus suffered. It wasn't just that Marcus appreciated Titus taking care of his mother. Titus had become a dear friend whom Marcus trusted. When Titus became very sick, Marcus started to reach out to the community to find help.

The friends he had made suggested some of the local people who helped families with healing. They also mentioned some of the Greek residents, mostly slaves, who were talented in medicines. But no matter what he tried, Marcus could not find any effective help for Titus.

Finally, Marcus asked the Jewish leaders if there wasn't some other help possible. That was when one of the leaders mentioned that there was a man traveling around the country that he had heard of, by the name of Jesus. He explained that some people claimed Jesus could heal people. The reason the man mentioned Jesus, he went on, was that Jesus was in Capernaum at the moment.

The challenge was that, according to his Jewish friend, Jesus had come only to help Jews.

Marcus did not let that deter him. He asked around and found where Jesus was speaking. Marcus was impressed by what he heard. He waited until Jesus was taking a break from speaking to crowds of people. Marcus was close to tears when he spoke to Jesus, explaining that Titus was at home paralyzed and in torment, and pleaded for Jesus to help.

Jesus, to Marcus' surprise, said He would come and heal him. At that, Marcus felt the humility of who he was, and the wonder of Jesus' willingness. He said to Jesus, "Lord, I am not worthy for You to come under my roof, but just say the word, and my servant will be healed. For I also am a man under authority, with soldiers under me; and I say to this one, 'Go!' and he goes, and to another, 'Come!' and he comes, and to my slave, 'Do this!' and he does it."

It was clear that Jesus had not heard anyone say that to Him before. He was so amazed that He talked to those around, using Marcus' comments as a witness of what He said faith really was.

Then He turned to Marcus and said, "Go; it shall be done for you as you have believed."

Marcus was overwhelmed with joy, thanked Jesus, and set off home with a sense of amazement at this land to which he had come. When he got home, Titus was the one who greeted him at the door, telling him he was completely well!

Titus asked if he might know where Marcus had gone. So, Marcus explained what he had heard about Jesus, and how he had gone and pleaded with Jesus for help.

Titus was amazed that Marcus had gone to a Jewish preacher for help, so Marcus told explained it this way. First Marcus told Titus a story about a centurion who was trying to help one of his soldiers. The soldier was having trouble with authority. He kept looking at orders he received and then tried to decide if they were right and whether he agreed with them. The centurion explained that wasn't his job. Soldiers have a certain limited authority, the centurion had said. Centurions have a different limited authority. And other more senior officers have their authorities. Each is responsible in their own areas of authority. A soldier is not responsible to decide the wisdom or correctness of orders he receives from officers who have greater authority.

Titus smiled and said, "You really told that soldier, sir!" Marcus replied, "You misunderstand. I was the soldier."

While Titus was wide-eyed in amazement, Marcus continued, "That was how I came to trust Jesus to heal you. I listened to those who sent me to Jesus. I listened to Jesus. And I knew."

"What did you know, sir?" said Titus. "I knew he had the authority," Marcus said. "Authority over what, sir?" asked Titus. Marcus paused, and then he said with a sense of wonder, "Authority over everything."

Titus found himself spluttering, "But you said no one had authority over everything!"

Marcus replied, "I know. I was wrong. Isn't it wonderful?"

21. A Funeral Attitude?

Sheime, his sister, and his mother and father thought of themselves as a close family. They enjoyed spending time together.

As Sheime was growing up, he enjoyed the holy days. That's when his family would have great celebrations. There were rituals that his sister Asna would explain to him (after his father had given him the official version). There was singing they all enjoyed (and which Nache, his mother, did very well). And there were special foods (Sheime liked the food).

There was one problem with the celebrations as far as Sheime was concerned. His family would talk about dead people.

They would talk about parents, grandparents, aunts, uncles they had known and loved. They seemed to enjoy talking about them and remembering things they had said and done, even though they were (from Sheime's point of view) dead and gone.

Sheime found it very frustrating listening to the conversations about dead people. After all, what good was it to talk about people you couldn't see or hear or be with. What good was it to remember things that had happened long ago. They were gone. What difference did it make to life being lived today. That's what Sheime thought, anyway.

The first experience with death, personally, that Sheime had was when his grandfather died. Sheime had visited his grandfather a few times. He hadn't known his grandfather very well. One memory he had was that his grandfather had drunk a strange smelling drink that Sheime tried one time. (Tasted terrible, he thought.)

His grandfather had been close to the family. There was a hole in the family with him gone. Others in the family talked about him and what he was like. They talked about things he had said and done. They shared their memories of him. Asna talked about visiting him and helping him. Sheime's father talked about the things Grandfather would have done and things he would have said.

But it all seemed strange to Sheime. His grandfather was dead. He was gone. There seemed no point to go on remembering things said and done, experiences, feelings from the past. It wasn't now. It wasn't real. What a waste of time!

Of course, Sheime and his sister Asna had regular arguments. Some were just normal brother and sister stuff. Some, though, were when she would say, "Well, Grandpa used to say…" Then Sheime would get angry and say, "I don't care what Grandpa used to say! He isn't here anymore! Let go of all that!" That's when Asna would let him alone and go find something else to do.

Sheime enjoyed spending time with his friend Levik. Levik was a good listener. Sheime would start spouting about his frustrations and Levik would listen. As Sheime went on, he would notice that the corners of Levik's mouth were turning up in an almost smile. Sheime would try to sound more serious, but then he would break into laughter when Levik started laughing.

Levik would try telling Sheime about his grandmother who had died a year ago. "Why do you remember her?" Sheime asked. "Well," Levik said, "I can remember the funny hat she wore. I remember the bread she baked. It was terrific! Even the Passover bread without yeast—really great! It's fun for me to remember how she enjoyed my loving what she made." Sheime just shook his head. "I don't get it."

It was when Sheime was a teenager that his sister got sick. She had had times when she had coughs. She seemed to have trouble when trees started to bloom in the spring. This time she couldn't get over it. Sheime spent time with her helping to take care of her. But then one night Asna kept getting weaker, and by morning she had died. Sheime was crushed, but he wouldn't talk about it. He closed a door in his mind and left Asna and all thought about her behind.

Levik tried to comfort him, but he was closed. He didn't want to remember. He found the funeral a ritual that didn't touch him. Year after year, he went on, unwilling to hold any memories of Asna or any other relative.

Then when his father died some years later, he didn't even want to go to the funeral. He helped his mother. He worked hard to support her. But he didn't want to have a past. He didn't want to have memories. He only wanted a future.

Levik spent time with Sheime and his mother. He tried to bring the warmth of remembered blessings in the past. Sheime wouldn't have it. When Levik and his mother reminisced, Sheime just got angry and left.

At work and at home Sheime started to have trouble with chest pains. He was more careful in what he ate and drank, but he couldn't get the pains to get better. He tried resting more but his mother grew more and more worried about him.

When it seemed that Sheime's future was getting short, he talked to Levik and his mother and told them he didn't want a funeral. Just get on with their lives, he told them. That was all he wanted for them.

When he died, Sheime's mother and Levik and his family planned a funeral and many of their neighbors came just because they knew Sheime's attitude and felt sorry for him and his mother.

As the funeral procession was heading for the burial spot, and as Sheime's mother, Nache, was deep in grief, a large group of people approached the procession. The procession slowed as the leader of the group came up to Nache. She looked up as the man said, "Do not grieve." The leader, Jesus, touched the coffin and the procession came to a stop. Jesus spoke to Sheime in the coffin, "Arise!"

In a very long couple of seconds, some people wondered if they should tell the man not to interrupt the procession, not to talk to the widow, and not to talk to the dead man, when Sheime sat up in the coffin!

To the amazement of the crowd Sheime started talking, "Who said that? What happened? Wait..." Jesus gave Sheime back to his mother, and Nache and Levik began explaining to Sheime that Jesus had talked to him as if he could hear him. Sheime said, "I did hear him! And...I was dead. So...is it true? There is life? I mean after death? There is hope? His words reached me! I died feeling hopeless and empty. And He reached into my emptiness and brought me to Life! This isn't the life I had before—this is real Life!"

Sheime went on talking to himself, "I guess there is hope in funerals. There still is the joy of Living. Living without end. Wow! Good memories go through death! There is a reason to remember! How really amazing!"

Sheime looked over and Jesus and his followers were heading off. Sheime ran over to Jesus and said, "Jesus! Thank You! Lord, thank You for another chance! Wow! Lord! What can I do for you?"

Jesus had turned to Sheime. He smiled and paused for a moment, looking at Sheime. Then He said, "Remember Me."

"Ah! Right, Lord! Got it! I'll remember You. I'll remember. From now on I'll remember! Especially You," said Sheime with more enthusiasm than he had expressed in any time in his previous lifetime.

The crowd was truly amazed and people were saying, "God has come and appeared to His people!" Others were staring open-mouthed. One said, "I've never been to a funeral like this! I might get to like funerals."

Sheime was running back to his mother and Levik, "Mom!" he shouted, "tell me about our relatives! Tell me the memories! Tell me the blessings! I've got a lot to catch up on!"

Levik said, to no one in particular, "Now that's a great funeral attitude."

22. Sorry for?

Her mother died when she was young. Her childhood, when she gave thought to it, had been difficult.

Her father worked hard to provide for her and her sister. He did his best to raise them, but he never seemed comfortable trying to prepare them for their life ahead after his wife died. When her sister got married the burden on her father eased.

But then her father suddenly died. Her world seemed to get cold and forbidding. She didn't know what to do. There were people who helped with the funeral, but the morning after the funeral seemed to be the edge of nothing. Her older sister had never been close to her because she said their parents always loved their youngest best. What her sister had actually said to her was, "This will be good for you—to see what it's like to be begging."

But begging hadn't worked. What worked was giving men satisfaction.

They were usually not very nice men. They were men who didn't care about her at all. What made it worse was that everyone knew! No one would talk to her. Except, that is, for women in the same situation. She had never known much about this part of the world, and now this was the only world she knew.

There was one of these women who befriended her. Yachna would talk to her and give her pointers on how to survive. "I'll call you Tirtza," she had said. "That's not my name," the woman had said. "That's just as well," Yachna had replied.

The days and months turned into years, and there seemed no hope for anything but more of the same.

Then one day, she heard of a prophet that was talking to large groups of people. Maybe I can get lost in the crowd and hear what he has to say, she thought. So, she went off to the edge of town to listen.

The prophet, Jesus his name was, had some very direct things to say to people who did not accept him. He invited people to believe that he had come to bless them. The woman especially remembered his words, "Come to me all you who are weary and burdened, and I will give you rest!" The words were a light to her in the darkness in which she was living. They seemed amazing and wonderful! Could this be real, she wondered?

Yachna started referring to him as "your Jesus". "Not my Jesus," she had told Yachna, "he has come for everyone." "Right," Yachna had said, "for women like us. Right. I doubt it." But the woman had not doubted it. While it was amazing to her, her heart had been touched.

It was about that time that Simon, a well known Pharisee, was at a meeting of many of his fellow Pharisees. They were in fact discussing this prophet, Jesus. "Why doesn't he see who we are?" Simon had said. "We are the people he should be socializing with." "Why don't you invite him to dinner, then," said one of the others. "Invite a few of us to come, too. Let him know that we are the important people he needs to be working with. He needs to have us on his side. And, really Simon, you have a great house and a great staff of servants." So that's what Simon did.

It was a couple days later that Yachna told the woman, "Your Jesus is coming to a dinner in town this week. House of Simon! Really big stuff, he is!" "He's not my Jesus," the woman said, "but how do you know?" "I heard it from some

of the servants at the market. You should go and see him."
The woman said, "Why are you telling me?" Yachna replied,
"You've been moping around…, no, well you've been
different since you saw him. You should go." "How could I
possibly get into a Dinner Party?" "Well," Yachna said, "I
have some friends in his servants. I think we could manage
it."

The night came, and Yachna saw that the woman had a jar
of something that smelled heavenly. "Where did you get
that!?" she said. The woman hesitated, then said, "I've been
saving a little, hoping to get out of this life." "You must have
spent it all!" "Well, yes, I did." "OK, Tirtza, let's do this!"

Yachna's friend met the woman at the back door and let her
wait inside until the right time.

Simon greeted Jesus with a lot of restraint when he came. It
had been a public invitation at a crowd of people, but now
that he was here, Simon didn't want his friends that were
already there to think that he liked Jesus. Jesus would just
be a guest among his honored friends.

Jesus looked like he was enjoying the dinner, but he didn't
seem very impressed. The dinner didn't appear to be
working. And Simon wondered who let in this woman at
Jesus' feet! What was she doing? Didn't Jesus know who
this woman was, after all! Couldn't he tell just by looking at
her? The other guests were getting restless and
uncomfortable.

Then, as if he heard what Simon was thinking, Jesus said, "I
have something to say to you, Simon." "Go ahead, Jesus,
tell me," Simon said. Now it was quiet. The guests were
listening. The woman was, too.

"A moneylender had two debtors: one owed five hundred
denarii, and the other fifty. When they were unable to repay,

he graciously forgave them both. (Simon thought that'll be the day!) So, which of them will love him more?" Simon answering said, "I suppose the one whom he forgave more." And he said to him, "You have judged correctly." (Simon smiled at that.) Turning toward the woman, Jesus said to Simon, "Do you see this woman? I entered your house; you gave me no water for my feet, but she has wet my feet with her tears and wiped them with her hair. (Simon was stirring uncomfortably as some of guests were also.) You gave me no kiss; but she, since the time I came in, has not ceased to kiss my feet. (Well if you were one of us, Simon was thinking!) You did not anoint my head with oil, but she anointed my feet with perfume. For this reason I say to you, her sins, which are many, have been forgiven, for she loved much; but he who is forgiven little, loves little." Then he said to her, "Rachel, Your sins have been forgiven."

"Forgives sins?!" some of the guests were saying to each other. But others were rather quiet as they began thinking about things they had said and done.

Simon said, "Forgiven little! Are you talking about me! I haven't done anything wrong! I don't need forgiveness!"

Tobias, Simon's business assistant, was thinking, You don't see the truth. If you don't want forgiveness, you don't get any.

Jesus said to the woman, "Your faith has saved you, go in peace. You believed me, and you believed that what you heard me say applied to you."

Simon had a slight purple tinge to his face now when he said, "Notice how he said I didn't have many sins…"

Tobias couldn't let it go on. He said, "He didn't say that. He said you didn't have much forgiveness because you don't want any!"

111

"What for!?? I haven't sinned! I'm not the one who has sinned here! After all, I'm a Pharisee!"

So Tobias went on, "Well he might be thinking of those houses you took away … from the widows I believe. Threw them out into the street to beg as I remember."

"That's just business! I don't need forgiveness!" Simon was beginning to shout now.

Then one of the guests joined in, "Well actually there was that deal you made with me when you said one thing but when it came to closing the deal it had changed—substantially in your favor as I remember." Several others were remembering some of Simon's crafty dealings with them rather loudly too.

Simon was spluttering now, "But those…"

"I'll pass on the dessert," said one of the guests, and the other guests were murmuring the same thing as they slowly got up to leave.

As Tobias was getting up to leave, he was saying to himself, "I've got to get a different job!"

Jesus and the woman got up to leave as well. Tobias came over and said to her, "What will you do now? You're not going back? Do you have anyone, any family?"

"Oh I have a sister," the woman said, "but she won't let me in for anything!"

Jesus leaned to her and said softly, "She will now."

The woman looked at Jesus with wonder, and even, finally, a sense of hope.

The servants looked at each other and started slipping away.

Leaving Simon. Alone.

23. The Neighbors

Mikhael was committed to God with all his heart. As a child growing up, worship was central to his life.

It wasn't just that his parents taught him to have a fervor for God and His word and His will. Somehow that just came naturally for Mikhael. He wanted to be close to God. Learning God's will was the satisfaction of his life.

Mikhael's father and their rabbi worked together to help him get a scholarship to law school. It was with great satisfaction that Mikhael learned the fine points of God's will in His word and in the interpretations of His word by famous rabbis and great lawyers in the past.

The mission Mikhael saw for himself was to help the people in his community to know and to apply God's will to every facet of life.

When he met Hannah, he knew she was the right woman to share his life and support his mission. She loved the Lord and truly cared about other people. They were married. They had a son, David, and all seemed to be going in the right direction.

Mikhael was teaching God's will and His compassion for His people. He was helping people apply God's law to questions and situations that came up in their lives, their work, their relations with other people.

The opportunity came up for Mikhael to serve on the local land board, dealing with ownership and legal testamentary distribution of land. Perhaps it was working with this sense of authority that brought a shadow of darkness into Mikhael's life.

He liked being important. He grew to like being in charge. He enjoyed other people looking up to him as an expert whom they respected. He was, after all, by now, an experienced lawyer. His focus was helping people believe correctly and act correctly.

At home, Mikhael took pleasure and pride in instructing their son, David. It's true that David was more interested in running around outside and spending time with other boys than Mikhael had ever been. At the same time, David accepted his father's instruction, and Mikhael was satisfied that David was on the right path of learning and might one day follow his passion for God's law.

There was some difficulty about some of the young people with whom David wanted to socialize. David had a clear perception of people based on what they liked to do and how much fun they were. Mikhael worked to explain that some people in their community had a history of marriage outside of God's chosen people. They had fellowship in meals with just anyone and were therefore not acceptable as ones with whom they could socialize. David was about to say, "Dad! You've got to be kidding!" when he saw that look on his father's face and realized it would be a very bad idea. Instead, he said, "I'll certainly give that some thought, Dad."

Mikhael took some satisfaction in that and considered it a step in the right direction. That is, until the day when David came home from school with what looked like a bandage wrapped around his elbow.

"What happened, David!?" Mikhael exclaimed.

"Oh, I'm ok, Dad. I was running on the way home and tripped where those stones are on the path, you know."

"Where did you get the bandage?"

"Well, Evra was with me, and his dad saw me fall down. So, he took me into their home and patched me up. He was really nice!"

"Do you mean Hezekiah?!"

"Yeah. I think that's what his mother said. They live just up the road a little way."

"David, those are not people with whom we can associate! Don't you remember me telling you that some people have a different background?"

"Right, Dad. But they were real nice, and I didn't actually associate much."

"No more of that! You need to stay away from them. I know their background."

David could see that this was a point where his dad wanted a definite yes, so he said, "Right Dad. Got it," and hurried off to get something to eat.

As Mikhael thought about it, he realized his concern really came from his work on the land board. He had received an application from Hezekiah to legally transfer ownership of a piece of property Hezekiah's father had owned in town. But Mikhael had done research on the family, and he knew that Hezekiah's wife, Mirkah, had a history that went back to the mixed marriages that occurred during the ancient time of the Captivity.

Mikhael's associate on the land board had asked him to find a way to legally deny the transfer of ownership so they could move this family somewhere else.

It was while Mikhael was doing research to find a legal way to deny the transfer, that he heard the news that there was a strange prophet visiting the town. The prophet, Jesus, had been traveling through the country telling people his new understanding of God's will. This might be the chance to take another step higher in authority and respect in town, he thought. I'll see how he does, talking to an experienced lawyer!

He found where Jesus was speaking and had a chance to talk to him. Mikhael started with a direct question that might give him a chance to show how foolish Jesus was compared to an educated lawyer. But when he asked, "Teacher, what shall I do to inherit eternal life?" Jesus said to him, "What is written in the Law? How does it read to you?" This wasn't exactly the opening that Mikhael was looking for, but he responded with the appropriate quote from the law that was taught to young people, "You shall love the Lord your God with all your heart, and with all your soul, and with all your strength, and with all your mind; and your neighbor as yourself."

While Jesus told him "You have answered well, do this and you shall live," (which Mikhael, of course, knew), an idea came to him. "Here is my opening," he thought. So, he pressed on with Jesus by saying, "And who is my neighbor?"

At this point, Jesus went off into a story in a Rabbinic style, about someone who got attacked along that difficult road up the mountain to Jerusalem. Mikhael could understand the point of view of the priest and the Levite in the story, and he wasn't sure where Jesus was going. But then, Jesus brought in the Samaritan.

Mikhael was about to break in and tell Jesus how ridiculous that was, when suddenly he felt his knees getting weak and his heart had a terrible twinge as he remembered what Hezekiah had done for David.

When Jesus got to the end, Mikhael realized that Jesus knew a lot more about applying God's law and maybe about him than he had thought.

Jesus then asked him, "Which of these three do you think proved to be a neighbor to the man who fell into the robbers' hands?" All Mikhael could think of to say was, "The one who showed compassion to him." Then Jesus said to him, "Go and do the same."

Jesus moved on to talk to others while Mikhael stood there thinking about what had happened. His idea of showing how knowledgeable and important he was had faded away. He felt the rigid container in which he carried the will of God in his heart and mind start to crack open, and he remembered early in his education learning that God gave His law, His expression of His will, to show His compassion to His people.

To use God's law. To be in His will. And to show God's compassion. Was it possible, he wondered.

By the time he got home, he realized he had to do something that was going to be seriously difficult.

Mikhael found Hannah and David at home and told them, "Come with me. We're going to visit someone." Both Hannah and David were mystified at being included in this visit. Then when David realized where they were going, he said, "Dad, you're not going to hurt anybody are you?"

Mikhael didn't seem to hear; he was focused on approaching Hezekiah's home. When Hezekiah came to the door he said, "This is a surprise!" Mikhael said, "I have come to thank you. I know it has taken a while for me to come. I'm sorry. You have been neighborly to us, and I have been stuck in a box of legalities without seeing the compassion from which they came."

Hezekiah smiled and said, "You're welcome. Thank you, very much for coming. Will you please come in? We were just about to have a meal. We have plenty. Will you join us?"

Mikhael could hear his wife's sudden gasp behind him. He said, "Yes, on condition that you come and enjoy dinner with us also, soon. And I'll take care of that land transfer for you," he continued with a mutter to himself, "and then I've got to get off that land board!"

As they reclined to eat, Hezekiah watching him asked Mikhael what he was doing. "Holding my breath, waiting to see if the general fabric of reality as I have come to know it will suddenly crack and crumble into small pieces." Then he smiled and sighed. Everyone relaxed as the room was filled with laughter.

Appendix of References

1. What Happened
      Luke 1.5-25, 1.57-80

2. The Visit
      Luke 1.39-56

3. A Sheep Story
      Luke 2.1-20

4. Anna's Reason
      Luke 2.21-40

5. Strange Gifts
      Matthew 2.1-12

6. The Student's Parents
      Luke 2.41-52

7. A Fisherman's Change
      Matthew 3.1-12, Mark 1.1-8,
      Luke 3.1-18

8. Next in Line
      Matthew 3.13-17, Mark 9.1-11
      Luke 3.21-22

9 His Smile
      John 2.1-12

Printed in Great Britain
by Amazon